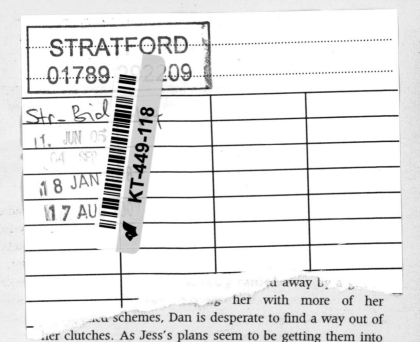

away by a g

her with more of her
schemes, Dan is desperate to find a way out of
her clutches. As Jess's plans seem to be getting them into
more and more trouble, Dan has to find a way to save them
both—and a way to finally break away from Jess . . . if that
is what he really wants . . .

Michael Harrison was born in Oxford in 1939. He has taught in
North Queensland, London, Oxford, and Hartlepool but is now
retired and enjoys visiting schools as a writer. He is married and
has two grown-up sons. His previous books include a history of
witches, funny novels, retellings of Norse myths, a book of poems,
Junk Mail, and a retelling of *Don Quixote*. *Carried Away* is his fourth
novel for Oxford University Press.

DISCARDED

Carried Away

Other Oxford books by Michael Harrison

Junk Mail
Don Quixote
It's My Life
Facing the Dark
At the Deep End

Carried Away

Michael Harrison

OXFORD
UNIVERSITY PRESS

OXFORD
UNIVERSITY PRESS

Great Clarendon Street, Oxford OX2 6DP

Oxford University Press is a department of the University of Oxford.
It furthers the University's objective of excellence in research, scholarship,
and education by publishing worldwide in

Oxford New York
Auckland Bangkok Buenos Aires
Cape Town Chennai Dar es Salaam Delhi Hong Kong Istanbul
Karachi Kolkata Kuala Lumpur Madrid Melbourne Mexico City Mumbai
Nairobi São Paulo Shanghai Taipei Tokyo Toronto

Oxford is a registered trade mark of Oxford University Press
in the UK and in certain other countries

British Library Cataloguing in Publication Data available

ISBN 0 19 271907 6

1 3 5 7 9 10 8 6 4 2

Typeset by AFS Image Setters Ltd, Glasgow
Printed in Great Britain by Cox & Wyman Ltd

This book is for
Tony and Rosemary

1

'I won't be a moment, Dan,' Dad said.

I was suddenly cold. Dad had left the car door open, as he always did. When I'd complained about it last time he'd just laughed and told me not to fuss so, said it wasn't worth bothering about for a few minutes. What did I think was going to happen: an armed gang swooping down while he was buying fish and chips? He didn't realize how quickly the temperature dropped. I undid my seat belt, wrapped the car rug round me, and lay flat on the back seat. I pulled the fringed end over my head so that I was in a warm cocoon.

I pretended I wasn't there and ignored the body moving into the car, the shutting of the car door. If Dad persisted in leaving the door open, even though he knew I didn't like it, then I certainly wasn't going to sit up and talk to him. The engine started with a roar and the car jerked away from the kerb. Dad was normally a careful driver. This was the sort of driving he did when he was in a real temper. It would be best to lie quiet for a bit and let him calm down.

I don't want to give the impression Dad was bad tempered or inconsiderate. Normally he was pretty reasonable but just occasionally he cracked. Tonight looked as if it could be one of those times. He got tired at work and then, when Mum was on nights, he had to get us a meal. I knew when things were getting on top of him because we'd have fish and chips: no cooking, no washing up. Mostly fish and chips was it, as far as it went. Stage two of his cracking up was him niggling at me. Leaving the car door open might have been habit, or he might have done it to get at me. 'Don't fuss about things that don't matter,' he'd say. He always wanted to improve me when he was tired. Just sometimes, just for a few minutes, he got really mad.

He was certainly in a real temper this time. The car jerked, the engine complained, and the steering was erratic. He had been cheerful enough as we were driving along; he loved going out for fish and chips and eating them in front of the telly. Something must have happened in the chip shop to annoy him. Come to think of it, I couldn't smell the fish and chips. Don't say he'd left his wallet behind again.

There was muttering and swearing in the front of the car in a voice that didn't sound like Dad at all. I pulled the rug off my face and looked cautiously out.

It wasn't Dad driving.

I lay absolutely still and stared at the back of the head of the driver above me. It wasn't Dad: smaller, darker, somehow just not Dad.

I had been abducted, carried away.

You shouldn't joke about things as Dad had last time. OK, it wasn't a gang and I didn't know if he was armed, but the car had been swooped down on, as Dad put it. Yes, I had this totally rational conversation in my head while I lay there wrapped up in the rug while some nutter jerked and swerved our car along the road.

But the driver surely didn't know I was in the car. If I said nothing and didn't move I would be quite safe, wouldn't I? This must be a car theft, an unplanned, opportunist car theft because Dad had, as usual, against my advice, left the door open and the keys in the ignition. It was his fault because he just wouldn't listen.

The car thief must be going somewhere. When he stopped he'd get out. I must be ready to make a run for it. If Dad had bought me a mobile as I asked him I'd have been all right. I could dial 999 now and speak quietly under the rug and under the engine noise or send a text message in silence. He just laughed when I asked for one. He said we couldn't afford one, that they were a rich kid's toy, that I was paranoid. I'd been right, though.

In some strange way I felt very calm and absolutely terrified at the same time. I was terrified of the car crashing; the driver seemed a total incompetent and I didn't dare put my seat belt back on. I never feel safe unless I am belted up. I told myself that I wouldn't fly through the windscreen like they show you on the telly as I was lying down. My angle of projection would be wrong. The worst that was likely to happen was that I would hit the front seats very hard, but they would cushion me. I was terrified of what he would do if he discovered me there. I'd read that burglars panic and lash out if they're cornered. Perhaps I should pretend to be dead, or asleep. I was terrified that I would be dumped in the middle of nowhere and that I'd freeze to death before morning. I was terrified that I had been kidnapped for some foul purpose.

I lay quite still and calmly watched myself being terrified. I was two people, an observer and a victim, neither of them at all practical. There wasn't actually anything practical I could do that I could think of. Did you expect me to hit the driver over the head with a spanner and grab the steering wheel before we crashed into the other traffic? Or perhaps you think I should have stuck a packet of Polos into the driver's back and said, 'This is a gun. Do exactly what I say'? Lying quietly under the rug was the only thing I could think of to do. It was, anyway, the only thing I could do. Even if I'd had a tube of Polos I don't think I could have sat up. I certainly couldn't have spoken; my throat had closed up tightly.

Lying in the back of the car felt like being on a bombing raid in one of those war films. Street lights and car headlights lit up the inside of the car like searchlight beams and then darkness came back, then lights again. There was the groaning of our engine and other noises in the night sky outside. This will end, I said to myself, this will end.

I will wake up in the morning in my own bed and come downstairs and Mum will be back from the hospital, sitting in the kitchen in her nurse's uniform eating toast. She'll be tired but pleased to see me. Dad will have gone to work already as he starts at eight so it will just be the two of us. She'll get my breakfast and see me off to school, checking that I've got everything, trotting out the usual warnings.

The car stopped suddenly in a well of darkness. The driver turned off the engine. There was silence, just broken by the intermittent clicks that metal makes while it cools down. I lay there, not daring to move, waiting, worrying that I might have to do something, make a decision, run for it with some man running after me across the fields and through the hedges.

The driver started laughing and saying, 'Yes! Yes! Yes!' I sat up in astonishment.

The driver was a girl.

2

'Who are you?' she said. She'd turned round as I sat up and stared at me. She looked as surprised as I felt. She must have been about the same age as me, though you can't always tell.

'It's my car,' I said, finding my voice at last.

'Your car? Bit young to drive, aren't you? Or was that your chauffeur I saw going into the takeaway? Little Lord Fauntleroy, are we?' She started laughing again, laughing at me, and I hated her.

'It's my dad's car. You knew what I meant.'

'Say what you mean and mean what you say,' she said. 'So, your dad's car?'

'He'll have rung the police and they'll be after you.'

'The entire Thames Valley police force looking for your dad's car—come off it.'

'They'll be looking for me,' I said. 'Child goes missing, that's always a priority.'

'You've got a point,' she said.

She pulled a mobile phone out of her pocket and if I hadn't hated her before I would have hated her then. She passed it back to me. 'Ring him up. Tell him you're all right.' I held it in my hand and stared at it. I didn't like to tell her I had no idea how to use it.

'He won't be at home,' I said. 'He'll be at the police station.'

'Ring his mobile then.'

'He hasn't got one.'

She stared at me and I could see what she was thinking:

some pathetic no-hoper family. Old car, no mobile, wimp son. OK, if she was so brilliant what was she doing stealing our old car anyway?

'Where do you live?' she asked. 'I'll take you home.'

'I don't want you to drive; you're not safe.'

'You drive,' she said.

'I can't.'

I looked out of the window and saw where we were and nearly laughed. We'd only come about a mile from the chip shop and were down a farm track about four hundred metres from home. Although I live in Oxford there's a belt of land with the canal and the railway line and some swampy fields that flood between the main suburbs and the villagey bit where we live. There's a track that runs from the road just before the bridge that crosses the canal and the railway through some fields and then crosses the canal at a swing bridge. The girl had driven the car along this track into the dark.

'I'll walk from here,' I said.

'Me too,' she said. She paused and then said, 'What are you going to say?'

'What do you mean, what am I going to say? I'm going to say what happened.'

'Won't that make you look a bit silly?' she said. ' '"Well, officer, I let this girl get into my dad's car and drive it away. No. I didn't try to stop her or to attract any attention. When she stopped I walked home. No, I didn't try to hold on to her, or shout for help, or find out who she was." Sounds good, doesn't it? Great headlines in the newspapers: BOY HERO DOES ABSOLUTELY NOTHING.'

'Who are you?' I said, and kicked myself as soon as I'd said it. The girl just started laughing again and I found I had stopped being frightened at some stage and was now losing my temper.

'I'll tell you what to say,' she said when she stopped laughing. 'Stick to something like the truth. You were lying

6

down in the car when it was driven off. It was so well driven you thought it was your dad. Then you sat up and the driver saw you, pulled off into here, opened the door and ran off. It was a man, of course, but you didn't see anything of him in the dark except the back of his head.'

As she finished she opened the car door and ran off, laughing.

Stupidly, oh, so stupidly, I did what she suggested.

SHOCK FOR CAR THIEF

The man who stole Keith Gedding's Ford Fiesta last night took more than he bargained for.

Mr Gedding had gone into Fresh Fry, the Summertown fish and chip takeaway, to collect supper for himself and his son Daniel.

While he was waiting to be served he saw his car being driven rapidly away. He rushed out of the shop but it had turned down South Parade and was out of sight.

The police were rung and the hunt was on.

What the thief hadn't realized was that Daniel was in the back of the car.

'I was lying down in the car when it was driven off,' Daniel said when I interviewed him at his parents' home in Lower Wolvercote. He smiled, 'It was so well driven that I thought it couldn't be Dad! Then I sat up and the driver saw me, pulled off into the track along Goose Green, opened the door and ran off. I couldn't see anything of the man in the dark except the back of his head.'

Daniel ran home and found his father there with a policeman. The car was found undamaged where it had been left.

'I'll be glad to get back to school,' Daniel quipped.

'That's the last time I leave the keys in the ignition,' Keith Gedding said.

Daniel's mother, Valerie, knew nothing of all the excitement until she arrived home from her night shift at the John Radcliffe Hospital where she is a nurse.

A police spokesman said they have no leads and are appealing to the public. 'Someone must have seen something,' Inspector Mopper said.

Oxford is suffering from a spate of car thefts. This is the third this week. Police urged drivers to look after their cars. 'A moment's carelessness is all a thief needs. This one ended happily. It might easily not have,' Inspector Mopper said.

When I read the report in the local paper I thought it was over and settled. There was no way the police were going to catch my particular car thief. Mum and Dad had been very delicate towards me. I think they expected me to wake up with nightmares, screaming and sweating in the middle of the night. I didn't, not then. Things settled down to the sort of normal life that makes boring reading.

It was about two weeks later, on the Monday of half-term, that I answered the phone one day. I was alone in the house: Dad was at work and Mum had gone shopping, asking me if I was sure I would be all right several times. She had become really paranoid about me since I had been carried away. It made me realize how closely supervised I had always been, how they had always known exactly where I was and what I was doing. My life was like those people who are let out of prison but have to be electronically tagged. I started to feel I wanted a bit of freedom, a life that was at least partly my own.

'Hello, Daniel,' the voice said.

'Dan,' I said (I'm fussy about that). 'Who is that?'

'Your private chauffeur,' the voice said and it was suddenly horribly familiar.

'Mum!' I shouted. There was no way I wanted to talk to this maniac.

'Your mother's out,' she said, 'and don't put the phone down or I'll ring back at a more embarrassing time.'

'How do you know Mum's out?'

'Look out of the window.'

Across the road there was a girl on a bicycle, sitting on the saddle and chatting into her mobile. It was just an everyday sight, nothing suspicious.

'How did you find me?' I asked.

'People who want to stay hidden don't get splashed all over the newspaper, or have their names in the telephone directory. Now listen, I don't want to hang around here.

Meet me in ten minutes by the canal lock.' She rang off and I watched as she cycled down the road. She didn't look at the house or wave. I let the net curtain drop. Best to go and see what she wanted, I thought. Best to leave a note for Mum saying I'd gone for a walk in case she got back before I did and worried. That would only increase the surveillance.

The girl was sitting on the long wooden arm of the lock gate, her bicycle propped up against it. As I came down the steps from the bridge she looked up and waved. There's nothing she can do to hurt me, I thought. Not in daylight. Not where there are people around. There was the usual fisherman hunched over his rod staring into the murk of the canal and a pair of old women waddling their fat dog along. Plenty of back-up, I thought.

She patted the arm next to her and gave me a piece of chocolate.

'Thanks for coming, Dan,' she said. 'I need your help with a little project I've got.' My heart sank. Somehow I knew this wouldn't be a school project on wild flowers along the canal bank.

'Thanks for the chocolate but no thanks,' I said. 'I'm not into projects and I don't want to help you. You've caused me enough trouble.'

'I don't think you have any choice,' she said. 'Telling deliberate lies to the police is a pretty serious crime. If I write that Inspector Mopper an anonymous letter telling him exactly what happened, in detail, he'll get you into the police station and third-degree you: lights in your eyes, not allowed to go to the loo, shouting, a quiet beating up— how long do you think you'd hold out against a professional?'

'You're bluffing. I'd tell him about you.'

She passed me another square of chocolate. I took it and said 'thanks', without realizing what I was doing.

'What's my name? Where do I live? Where do I go to school?' She suddenly put one cold hand over my eyes. 'Describe me.'

'Err . . . a bit taller than me, short dark hair, skinny, err . . . '

'How many girls in Oxford would that describe?' She took her hand away. 'You'd better have a good look. Make notes if you like.' She sat grinning at me. I felt stupid.

'What's your name?' She laughed and gave me more chocolate. 'What's the project?' I said, feebly.

'A little burglary,' she said.

I stared at her. She really was a nutter. 'Whose house?'

'Mine,' she said.

3

'You're mad,' I said. 'I'm not a burglar and I'm not getting involved with any of your silly games.'

She took a piece of paper out of her pocket and passed it over. It had been typed out on a computer and looked impressive.

To Inspector Mopper
Thames Valley Police

I have important information about the incident described on page 2 of the *Oxford Mail* of Friday 2nd February about a taking away of a car. The account given by Daniel Gedding is completely untrue. I know this because I took the car, and I told him what to say. He agreed to lie about the incident because he was afraid of looking silly.

It wasn't a man who took the car. I am a girl of Daniel's age. I took the car for a laugh. I know you may think that I am really a man and am just trying to stop you looking for me. When you receive this letter put a notice in the *Oxford Mail* saying that you are seeking further information and giving a phone number and I will telephone you on that number at exactly 3 p.m. the same day and you can question me.

'It's on disk, if you thought tearing it up would do any

11

good,' she said. 'You can keep that copy if you like. Put it in your scrapbook next to the newspaper cutting.'

How did she know Mum had cut it out and said she'd get me an album to put it in? 'I was right, wasn't I?' she laughed. 'Oh dear, how embarrassing it will all be for you. Much simpler if you just join my silly game, as you call it, especially as I've picked you for my side. Come on, say yes. It'll be a laugh.'

She certainly seemed cheerful, though perhaps hyped up might be more accurate. I stood up and walked to the edge of the lock and stared down. The water was at the lower level, a long way down.

'Don't jump,' she said. 'It won't be that bad, I promise.'

'I wasn't going to,' I said angrily. 'I just need to think.'

I hate being laughed at. Mum and Dad are very good and listen to what I say and take me seriously, but at school the nastier gang mock me, call me Pompous Old Prat, or Pop. I hate it and don't know how to answer. If I reason with them, as I've been told, they just laugh all the more and strut up and down in front of me doing what they think is a brilliant imitation of me. If I turn away they walk after me. There's no answer. Now this girl was sitting on the canal gate and about to make me the joke of all Oxford, and perhaps nationally as well. THE BOY WHO LET A GIRL STEAL HIS FATHER'S CAR—I could see the headlines. I could hear Mum's voice.

'What would I have to do?' I asked, my back to her still.

'Tomorrow evening,' she said. 'We're all going to Gran's.'

I turned round and looked at her. 'What's the point? What's going on?'

Her mobile rang and she cursed. 'Yes, Anna. Yes. OK. Yes.' She put the phone back in her pocket. 'My big sister. I've got to go. Have you got an e-mail address?'

I hadn't. Dad said we couldn't afford the phone bills. 'It's the Stone Age round here,' she said. 'Do you know the Museum of Modern Art café? Behind Marks? Be there at three, or else.'

She got on her bicycle and rode along the towpath towards Oxford, scattering dogs and old women as she went. I stared after her. Who was she? What on earth was going on?

I climbed up the steps towards the road. If I could get home before Mum saw my note she'd think I'd been in all morning and encourage me to go out. I'd have to tell her I was meeting a friend, and she'd want to know who and where and what we were going to do. I wasn't used to lying to her. I didn't think I'd be very good at it. It had been difficult about the car but I had been in a state then anyway and everyone just believed what I was saying. Lying in cold blood was different. I told myself that they'd driven me to it; it was the only way I could breathe.

It was all taken care of, taken out of my hands. I was reading in my room when the phone rang. After a bit Mum came up and knocked on my door and had a funny smile on her face. 'You didn't tell me you'd got a girlfriend, Dan. How long's this been going on? Said you weren't to forget you were going to the Museum of Modern Art this afternoon. I didn't know you were interested in art, especially that modern stuff. You are a dark horse. She sounded a nice girl, Jess.'

'She's not my girlfriend,' I said. At least I had half a name now. That narrowed the suspects down a bit. How many dark-haired skinny girls in Oxford were called Jess?

'You'll want a bit of extra money if you're courting,' Mum said and put a five pound note on the bed.

'I'm not courting,' I said. This wasn't like Mum. It sounded almost as if she was teasing me, but I picked the note up quickly in case she changed her mind. Money was tight in our house. I'd thought about doing a paper round but was quite glad when I was told I couldn't as it would make me too tired for school.

Mum went away and I felt I was a pawn in the hands of these women who were conspiring behind my back. What was going on? Did I know enough about this Jess now to stop her threats? But Jess seemed a very determined person and I didn't want anyone knowing I'd lied to the police.

The café was quite quiet when I found it. I'd not been there before and was a bit embarrassed walking down into the basement and opening the heavy door. I expected the room to be full of arty types who would all turn and stare at me but they seemed perfectly normal and no one took any notice of me. Jess was there already and had bought me a flapjack and a Coke. I sat down opposite her. 'Suppose I don't like these?' I asked.

'Then get your own and I'll have them. Actually, "Thank you" is more usual. I'm surprised your mother didn't teach you that; she sounded a very polite woman.'

'What were you doing, ringing up like that? Are you mad?'

'I'm in charge here,' she said. 'You're in my power. I'll decide what to do. I wanted to make sure you'd turn up. And you may need help getting out of the house tomorrow evening. I'm your excuse.'

'But you're going to your gran's, you said.'

She laughed at me. I hate that. 'It's a good thing I am in charge,' she said. 'You seem a complete prat.'

That made me really wild. I was fed up with people calling me a prat. I'd show her. I didn't need a girl to ask Mum if I could leave the house. I wasn't some wimp who couldn't do anything. 'What's the plan?' I said.

She looked a bit surprised at that. One up to me, I thought.

Then she told me.

She had broken her father's camera. He was a gadgets fanatic and had this state-of-the-art camera that could do everything, make toast even, she said, though I doubted that. He'd bought some new attachment that converted his film camera into a digital one so that he could link it to the computer. He'd had a digital one before but it didn't take such brilliant photos as his old camera, apparently. Jess had been curious, had a go with the digital camera when she was alone in the house and somehow bust it.

'Why not just say you're sorry?' That's what I would have done, though I couldn't imagine doing something as childish as that in the first place.

Apparently this wouldn't have been a good idea. In fact my even asking was the dumbest thing anyone had ever asked since questions were invented, which apparently was in the Old Stone Age and had something to do with a misplaced mammoth—it got a bit complicated around here and I lost track. Jess seemed to be someone who enjoyed getting carried away with her own words, whether they made much sense or not. Obviously, someone who asked such a question was pre-Old Stone Age in their mental powers, pre-Neanderthal in fact, pre-ape probably, almost certainly amoebic.

I let the question go.

Problem: the damaged camera. Solution: have it stolen by me.

The way Jess described it, hunched over her Coke across the table from me in the café, there was no other possibility. Some came to mind and foolishly passed my lips, only to be swatted with scorn by my opponent as they crossed towards her, though none, thank goodness, were quite as stupid as owning up apparently was. Putting it back and saying nothing and taking it away from the house and dumping it would both put immediate suspicion on her. It

15

gradually emerged, as I desperately tried to talk her into a solution that didn't involve me, that she had something of a history. This wasn't the first thing she'd fiddled with and broken. The list seemed to include watches, vacuum cleaners, dishwashers, burglar alarms, sewing machines, automatic garage doors, lawn mowers . . . It sounded as though our car had had a lucky escape. The punishments and dire warnings got more and more severe each time.

'Why do you do it then?' I asked.

Jess just couldn't believe anyone could be as totally gormless as I obviously was and have so far escaped serious accident. She was surprised I was actually allowed out on my own and really began to wonder if I was actually capable of such a simple task as the one I was needed for. This was fine by me but I really couldn't understand why she found my questions quite so silly. I thought they were pretty shrewd. I let her words wash over me and concentrated on feeling wise.

Eventually she sat back in her chair and pulled out a notebook. She tore a piece of paper from it and passed me a pencil. 'I'll dictate the instructions to you,' she said. 'It's important that nothing links me to the crime.'

I thought it was pretty important that nothing linked *me* to the crime, but I didn't say it out loud. It was probably a stupid thought.

4

I crouched behind the front hedge feeling sick and needing the loo. I had my instructions in my hand and kept staring at them in the light of the lamp-post across the road, but they made no sense. Go, go, go, I kept telling myself but somehow going felt as if it needed more courage than I had.

There is no danger, I said to myself firmly. The burglar alarm is broken. They've been too busy to get round to having it mended. Jess has left a back window open, hidden by the curtains. They are all out. I had watched them drive off from the end of the road ten minutes ago. I told myself I was waiting in case they realized they had forgotten something and came back unexpectedly.

I had a plan of the downstairs of the house showing where the camera was kept. All I had to do was go through the window, go to the room the camera was in, pull open a few drawers on the way, take the camera, climb out of the window again, break the window, walk quietly away, drop the camera in the canal.

I had to break the window to show there had been a burglary. I had to break the window on my way out just in case any nosy neighbour was putting the cat out and heard something. Jess would leave a strip of sticky-back plastic she'd 'borrowed' from her school library on the window sill. I was to peel off the backing, stick it on the window and then hit it firmly with the stone she would have put below the window in the garden.

There was absolutely no danger and nothing could go

wrong. It had all been thought out by a mastermind. Unfortunately the mastermind had to use an amoeba-intelligence like me but the plan was so foolproof even a fool could cope with it.

That's what Jess had said in the café and she had convinced me at the time. It even sounded exciting, part of the new life I'd been longing for, the new me.

I was terrified.

A car came along the road, its headlights searching through the hedge making me feel exposed, obvious. I expected sudden braking, running feet, iron fingers on my shoulder. It drove past. Anyone who did see me would just think I was playing some game with my mates. Another car. It would be better to move than to stay crouched here. It would be. Definitely. Any minute now a dog-walker would amble along, his nosy hound sniffing me out.

I made myself straighten up, partly because I was getting cramp. Once I was standing up it was easier to move towards the back of the house. The lawn looked black; bushes loomed like accusing adults. I had a torch in my pocket, a small one Jess had given me, but didn't dare use it yet.

Once round the corner of the house I felt safer. It was darker and out of sight of anyone passing along the road. The neighbouring houses were level with this one which meant that if anyone was looking out they wouldn't see me. I just had to hope there were no gardeners so fanatical they weeded through the night.

I counted along. There was the window. Half a brick lay on the patio below it. I put my fingers out to the window, sweaty in the rubber gloves Jess had given me. We'd had an argument about them. I hate wearing gloves and rubber gloves make my flesh creep. I said it didn't matter about fingerprints because no one would know it was me—at least I hoped they'd never know. I didn't see how they could. Jess said it was important that there weren't any fingerprints as only an idiot would leave them, giving me one of her meaningful looks. She would wrap a handkerchief around her hand when she opened the window. 'And if you do leave prints, they'll know what size you are,' she'd said, making me feel small. So I was sweating inside rubber gloves.

One edge of the window was slightly sticking out. I pulled it towards me and there was a black hole waiting for me to climb through.

More accurately, to scramble ungainly, undignifiedly through. To entangle myself with curtains. To knock over a table on the other side and hear something break. To drop to the floor clumsily.

None of those were in my instructions.

Nor were my instructions any longer in my hand.

The night garden was suddenly attractive. I pulled the window shut in case someone noticed it was open and knew they were out. And it delayed the moment I had to step through into the nightmare ahead.

I took the torch out of my pocket and shone it on the floor. There were the instructions and the plan and there was the sheet of plastic. I parted the heavy curtains and went through, letting them drop behind me.

Light startled me, even though Jess had said there would be lights left on in some of the rooms. Somehow it made it worse.

Pieces of china were scattered on the floor. I had to stop myself picking them up. Out of this room, I had to go. Into the hall. Brightly lit by its overhead light so I felt as if I was on stage with an invisible audience out in tiers and watching me. First door on the left. This was shut and opening it was hard. White knuckles gripped the knob and turned it so slowly that minutes passed with no change visible. Only the pressure of the hall light finally pushed me in.

It was a small room. Facing me were curtains, closed across a window, with a desk in front: on it a computer with its scanner and printer and modem in an orderly line. The desk top was otherwise bare. Next to it, lit in the beam of light that came past me from the hall, was a chest of drawers. The chest of drawers. 'Top left-hand drawer' my instructions said as I checked them yet again. I was supposed to open all the drawers and rummage through. I'd better get on with it, I thought.

I took the camera out first. It was in a black bag with a wide strap, as Jess had described. I put it over my shoulder so that my hands were free. I pulled open the other drawers. Jess's father was obviously a very tidy man. I like being tidy. Mum isn't and she keeps on about not knowing where I get it from as if I'm some sort of freak. I say it's easier to find things, that I don't spend hours searching for something as she does frequently. That's not the reason, though. I just like to see things orderly, lined up in straight rows. Under control, Dad muttered once when Mum was going on about it yet again, and I suppose that's true. What's wrong with wanting to be in charge?

I wasn't in charge now. I was reluctantly following orders, driven by embarrassment and guilt, harnessed by a ruthless girl. I had to rummage through someone else's beautifully tidy drawers. Two of the drawers just held files. I took some out and dropped them on the floor. 'Look as though you were disturbed and left in a hurry,' Jess had said. Another drawer contained stationery and I didn't think I needed to disturb that. The last drawer was trouble. It contained all sorts of gadgets and things that were fascinating and desirable, like a miniature tape-recorder, and among them a digital stopwatch and pedometer, according to its case, that I really fancied. I thought of putting it in my pocket but knew it would be stealing. I shut my eyes, put my hand in and swirled it about.

I tipped the fancy adjustable desk chair over. That would surely do. Now I just had to get out and break the window. I'd locked my bicycle up by the canal so that I could drop the camera in and then cycle off like mad for home. I'd even worked out a diversionary route in case anyone was watching. They'd see me setting off in entirely the opposite direction and then I'd zigzag through the side streets home.

The window, I told myself. My instructions were very clear: I had written them down to Jess's instructions as she read off her copy, later torn up and put in the café bin:

- Get out with plastic.
- Close window.
- Peel off backing.
- Stick on glass by window catch—NB: <u>outside</u> of window, stupid! For goodness' sake! You don't have to write down every word.
- Bang once firmly with stone. (in fact it was half a brick)
- Open window wide again.

I eased the camera bag round so that it hung on my back out of the way. I went out into the lighted hall.

A window broke in one of the back rooms.

5

My first, stupid, thought was that Jess had decided she couldn't trust me and had come to take over.

My first, stupid, action was to run upstairs.

I know what I ought to have done. It's so easy when it's not happening to you. I should have checked which room the burglar was coming in. If it wasn't 'my' room I should have hidden behind the curtains and then climbed out of the window and run for it. If it was 'my' room I should have hidden behind the curtains in the other room, opened that window quietly, and climbed out and run for it.

I ran upstairs, silent on the carpet, and stood panting silently on the landing. There was silence below. The landing was dark. Below me there was a slice of brightly lit hall. Enough light came up the stairs for me to see I was surrounded by doors, some open, some shut. The nearest room had its door open and I could make out a bed, with enough room to crawl underneath.

I dropped to my hands and knees and as I did so the top of a head appeared below. I froze. A dark curly head. Not Jess.

The head moved out of sight again. A real burglar was not on my list of instructions.

My mind refused to work properly. Such stupid thoughts kept coming into my mind just when I needed to think clearly, and quickly. It was as if I was dreaming, or channel surfing. One programme was *Boy Hero Hour* and had me striding down the stairs and capturing the burglar and tying him up and receiving universal acclaim. Then it switched to *Nightmare House* and the timorous child was pursued from room to room and finally bloodily battered. *The Great Escape* had me climbing out of an upstairs window and edging my way down some convenient climbing plant. This shifted somehow into *Night in the Garden* with a discussion of the best plants to grow if you want a handy escape route.

I could hear the sounds of searching from downstairs. At least Jess won't be able to complain about me not doing my job properly, I thought. And then I thought, If the burglar takes other stuff, she'll think it was me. She'll think she has complete control over me then. No one will believe that she forced me into burgling her house. That was why she had made me write down the instructions to her dictation: my handwriting, my word against hers.

I forced my brain into some kind of order. No, I was not going to confront him. No, he was not going to attack me if I didn't threaten him. No, I was not going to climb out of a window. No, it was too risky trying to creep out of the house. No, Jess was no threat. What evidence would there be against me? I was wearing these horrid rubber gloves, I wouldn't have any of the stolen goods, and I would have destroyed my instructions. I was clearly not the criminal type.

I had another idea. I would put the camera bag under her bed and then hide until the burglar had gone. If Jess questioned me I would say that I had turned up, seen a real burglary in progress, and gone away, thinking that the burglar would do the job for me. No, I didn't know how the camera had got under her bed. Yes, it was bad luck her mother found it. Yes, I am sorry she's in such trouble. Go to the police if you want. They'll talk to your parents and learn you're in trouble at home. Poor little rich girl, they'll think.

Neat, I told myself, pretty good under pressure. She'd got me into this nightmare and she can suffer for it. My new instructions were simple: find Jess's bedroom, hide camera, hide self.

I leant cautiously over the bannister rail. There were sounds from the front of the house. I took the torch out of my pocket and shone it through the door next to me. The narrow beam picked out a neatly made bed, a chest, a chair. There was no clutter, no clothes draped anywhere or on the floor, nothing out of place. It must be a spare room.

Across the landing was the bathroom, then three more doors, and—I suddenly saw—a narrow stairway going up to what must be a loft conversion. I started to get panicky. The next room was her parents': double bed, their own bathroom, phone by the bed.

Phone!

I forgot all my other plans and went quickly across to the phone. I picked it up and squeezed under the bed holding on to it tightly. I had to take the camera bag off my shoulder and drag it under with me. The perfect escape route was now in my hands: dial 999 and wait for the police car.

And then explain what I was doing in the house.

There wasn't much room under the bed. I could move my head about ten centimetres off the carpet. The carpet was dusty. I had read enough books to know that if I lay in the dust under the bed I would sneeze just at the moment the burglar came into the room.

I pressed the buttons. 'Which service do you want, fire, police, or ambulance?'

'Police,' I whispered.

'There are serious penalties for hoax callers and all calls can be traced,' the voice said.

'Police. It's serious,' I whispered.

There was a pause and then the questions started again.

I had to whisper. I had to listen very carefully at the same time in case the man was creeping silently up the carpeted stairs towards me.

In the end I just repeated the address and whispered, 'Please help; I'm so frightened,' and put the phone down. I peered through the slit in front of me, trying to keep my nose out of the dust. The landing was shadowy in the light that came up the stairs. The house was quiet.

I lay there and thought of my problems. I had to avoid the burglar. Staying under the bed was probably the best thing to do. It was certainly the easiest. I had to avoid the police, if they came. Staying under the bed was probably safe. I had to avoid Jess's parents. Staying under the bed was definitely not a good idea. If my house was burgled, looking under the bed was the first thing I'd do, and I'd do it while the police were still in the house.

Hiding under Jess's bed looked the best bet. She'd look under her bed and somehow get me out of the house. But suppose she screamed? And what time would I get home? I was supposed to be back by ten. And what about fairly urgent problems like the loo?

My bladder decided it. The embarrassment of an accident surrounded by the police and Jess's family would be so horrendous that almost any risk was worth it. I edged slowly forward, listening intently, but all I could hear was my sweatshirt rubbing on the carpet as I moved.

I crept slowly, silently towards the doorway. My heart thumped, blotting out all other noises, or perhaps there just weren't any other noises. I forced myself through the doorway, on to the landing. A crash from downstairs made me jump, but it also gave me the courage to run across to the bathroom. He was still in the house, downstairs, and searching.

I closed the bathroom door quietly and slid the bolt. If he tried it he'd know I was here, but if he came in he'd hardly miss me anyway. Light from the street lamp outside came through the crinkled glass and lit the room enough for me to move around and I felt better after the loo.

There was an airing cupboard in the bathroom that was big enough for me to squeeze into. It might be best to unlock the bathroom door and hide in there. I didn't know a lot about burglars but I didn't think he'd spend time in the bathroom. But perhaps people often hid valuables in an airing cupboard and it would be the first place he'd look upstairs. I dithered.

The bathroom lock was held on by three small screws. Worse, I realized that it was one of those safety ones you can open with a coin from the outside. Locking the door was the worst thing I could do. I slid the bolt back slowly and very gently turned the handle.

Inside my head I could see the man standing on the landing watching the handle turning slowly, waiting for me to step out.

A blue light flashed like an eerie lighthouse through the bathroom window. The police had arrived.

6

I did not want to get caught by the police. I opened the bathroom door and stepped out on to the landing. I was suddenly dazzled by a bright light in my face. I put my arms up to cover my eyes.

The doorbell shrilled through the house. The light left my face, was switched off. I saw the burglar standing halfway up the stairs looking straight at me in horror as if I was the person who had rung the bell. Then he turned and ran down the stairs. I heard a shout from the back and some crashing.

I came down the stairs moving from one step to another carefully, keeping to the wall. The sounds came from the back so it would be best to go out of the front. Once I was clear of the door I could just pretend I was a nosy passer-by, or I could run for it.

There was an inner door and then an outer hall with coats hanging up, and then the outside door. I put my hand on the door knob and turned and pulled. Nothing happened. I looked at the lock, thinking it must be like the one we had at home with a knob you turn. There was no knob to turn. There was a keyhole. There was no key.

I turned in the porch to go back into the hall. A policeman was walking towards me. I was trapped.

Somehow inspiration came to me. Perhaps Jess was a great teacher. I walked towards the policeman. 'Thank goodness,' I said. 'I rang you. He grabbed me.' And then, to my total embarrassment, I found I was crying.

It was the best thing I could have done, but I wished I hadn't. The policeman was immediately sympathetic. He said things that didn't make sense at first but then I realized that he thought I lived in the house, had been there when the burglar broke in. At first I thought I shouldn't explain, but then I realized that the truth would come out before long, as soon as Jess's parents came back, and that I had to say something now.

'He pulled me in,' I said, suitably incoherent.

'Take your time,' the policeman said, and passed me a tissue. I blew my nose and thought desperately.

'I came to see my friend. My friend Jess. She lives here. The door was a crack open. I thought that was a bit odd but it didn't worry me. I rang the bell. No one came so I pushed the door open and called out. "Hello!" or something. Then this man came and I said, "Is Jess in?" and he grabbed me and pushed the door shut.'

'Why are you wearing rubber gloves?'

I looked down at the bright yellow on the ends of my arms. My brain was in top gear, fortunately. 'That was a joke. Jess said don't come too early or her mum would make me do the washing up. So I put these on, as a joke.'

'So how did you manage to ring 999?'

I could see he was very suspicious of me and somehow this irritated me. Just then the other policeman came in and said the man had got away through the back gardens. He saw me standing there with rubber gloves on and said, 'Well, at least we've caught the mastermind.'

'He says he's a friend of the family,' my policeman said. 'He says he came to the house wearing rubber gloves as a joke, the door was open, he called out and the intruder pulled him in and let him dial 999.' He made it sound all rather implausible.

'It's true,' I said indignantly.

'The door's shut now,' the second policeman said. He walked into the porch and tried it. 'And it needs a key to open it. Odd, that. Did you see the intruder lock it?'

'Yes,' I said, hastily. 'He said he didn't want anyone else wandering in.'

'And where did he find a key?'

I felt things slipping away from me. The first policeman had seemed to believe me, but the second obviously didn't and he was winning. I didn't have answers to so many questions and I just couldn't think while they were asking so many. I couldn't even burst into tears to gain time.

'The key? Where did he put it?'

'I don't know. I was frightened. I didn't see.'

'And how did you manage to phone?'

'I did phone, didn't I?' Going on to the attack was all I could do. They'd lost the real criminal and they were now bullying me, the innocent victim. It was just typical. I tried to believe this so that I wouldn't just collapse and admit everything.

'There was a call from this address.'

'Why would I phone if I was part of the burglary?' This was my strongest defence. I had to keep repeating it.

'We're not accusing you, sonny,' my more sympathetic policeman said. 'We're just trying to sort out what happened here.' His radio started talking to him and he walked into the nearest room and shut the door. The second policeman stared at me in an unpleasant way, as if he knew I was guilty and was going to prove it.

The first policeman came out and asked me to describe the man. I nearly said I'd only caught a glimpse of him in the half light of the stairs after being blinded by his torch but I remembered just in time that this wasn't my story.

'About your height,' I said. 'Dark curly hair. Sort of normal, really.'

'Age?'

'I don't know. Grown-up.'

'What was he wearing?'

I screwed up my eyes trying to remember. 'Dark jacket, dark gloves. He just looked sort of dark all over.'

'Was he black?'

'No, white, quite pale really but with sort of designer stubble.'

He went back into the room to talk into his radio again. Number two stared at me and I looked down at the floor. We waited silently until the first policeman came out again.

'Now, sonny, we need your name and address. Are your parents at home?' He wrote down the details as I told him. It was no good making anything up. I knew they wouldn't let me just make my own way home. He went across to the phone on the hall table and dialled. I could hear Mum squawking as he explained who he was and where I was and that one of them would have to come and collect me now.

'She says you were going to your friend Ben who lives down your road,' he said when he'd finished.

'I was embarrassed,' I said. 'She thinks Jess is my girlfriend and teases me.'

There was a scratching sound in the front door and it opened. A man came in, and a woman, and three children, Jess, a bigger girl, and a smaller boy. There was a Babel of talk, everyone at once and then it became more orderly.

'Do you know this young man?' my policeman asked. 'He says he was invited here this evening.'

'No,' Jess's father said. 'I've never seen him before. He certainly wasn't invited.'

'Oh, Dan, I'm sorry,' Jess burst in. 'I forgot we were going out tonight.'

Everyone turned and looked at her and she went bright red. 'Dan's a friend,' she said. 'I invited him round. Is that illegal? Am I supposed to fill forms out in triplicate if I want to invite a friend to what's supposed to be my home?

Do my friends need to be vetted, checked up on in case they've got a police record or an infectious disease, or have failed to do well enough in their SATs? I would have thought it was possible just to say, ''Do drop in'' and then just forget. It's not really such a big deal, is it?'

Jess's brother and sister were making faces at each other as if this was yet another example of their embarrassing sister letting them down in public. Her mother started a very rational lecture on the right way to treat one's friends and her father took the policemen on one side and talked to them man-to-man. I stood there in my rubber gloves feeling totally stupid.

There was a ring at the door and Jess's father opened it. Mum and Dad, looking worried. Ten people in the hall. Chaos. Embarrassment. Questions. It seemed my story was accepted, at least for now, but I had to be brought to the police station tomorrow at ten o'clock, with a responsible adult. That would give me time to work out what to say.

Jess raised her eyebrows at me as I was going out. I yawned and pointed down and nodded at her. I hoped she'd understand what I meant. It was the best I could do in front of all those people. It wasn't enough for her. She came after me down the path. She held my arm and pretended to kiss me.

'The camera?'

'Under a bed.'

Mum laughed. 'You are a dark horse, Dan.'

If only she knew.

7

Jess rang me two days later. She said she knew my
parents were out and that I was to meet her in the
Museum of Modern Art café at half past ten.
'Debriefing,' she said.

It was a miserable day with sleety rain coming down,
so I caught the bus at the end of our road and watched the
world through the drops running down the glass.
Debriefing! I'd had enough questions to last me my
lifetime: Mum, the police, Mum. I still didn't know who
believed what. If I hadn't rung the police they certainly
wouldn't have believed me—but if I hadn't rung them they
wouldn't have been there—but if they hadn't been there
the man would have got me . . . It all went trickling damply
through my mind.

Mum believed me, but she believed too much. Somehow
the fact that I had lied about where I was going that evening
helped her spin great fantasies of her own. She believed in
this great romance between me and Jess. She'd quickly
learnt that Jess's parents, ''the Arbours'' as she kept calling
them as if they were royalty or famous, were stinking rich
and that Jess went to a private school and Mum was so
impressed by it all. She kept wanting to know how we
became friends, and I kept evading it, putting on the big
shy act, because (a) we weren't friends and (b) I couldn't
say that we had met in Dad's car when she stole it.

In a way I didn't dislike the thought of talking to Jess. I
wouldn't have to lie, to watch every word, to have to
remember what I'd said before so that I didn't contradict

myself too much. A bit of confusion was all right because you can get muddled in a stressful situation, and no one suggested nothing had happened. It was just that no one could quite believe my story, but so far they hadn't been able to disprove it.

Jess was there already. This time she had bought me a cappuccino and a slice of chocolate cake. I thought this was a bad sign: I needed softening up. She smiled at me in her "let's be best mates" way and waved grandly at the chair opposite her.

'Hi!' she said. 'You were brilliant the other night. Absolutely brilliant!' I sat down, suddenly pleased to see her. At last someone recognized how well I'd done in very difficult circumstances.

'You might have told me you'd laid on a second burglar,' I said. She laughed, and that made me feel good too. A couple of women turned and looked at her and I saw with their eyes this lively and really rather good-looking girl enjoying a joke with her boyfriend.

'The camera,' she said, and my brief pleasure evaporated. She nodded down at a Sainsbury's carrier bag by her chair.

'What about it? I did my best. I couldn't walk out with it in front of the police, could I?'

'You were brilliant,' she repeated. 'And I rescued it from under the bed before anyone found it, and Dad's listed it as stolen for the insurance. The thing is, it's got to be chucked and it's best if you do it.'

'Why?'

'Suppose someone saw me? I know it's not likely, but it is possible. It wouldn't matter if it was you. Please.' She widened her eyes and looked pleadingly at me. I hesitated, because I knew she was just manipulating me, and I didn't like it.

'I'll come with you,' she said. 'We'll do it now. The

canal's not far. The thing is, if I'm just with you it won't matter because you'll be carrying the bag. If I was carrying it some nosy person might ask me what was in it. Please.' The eyes widened, almost irresistibly.

The cake was delicious and I weakened and pulled the carrier bag towards me. When we came out of the café the sky had cleared and watery sunshine brightened the streets. We fought our way through the crowds and the traffic to the bridge where the canal begins. I said I would walk home along the canal and drop the bag in somewhere quiet but Jess said she'd come with me as far as her bridge and watch, 'for her peace of mind'.

The rain had kept the usual dog walkers from coming out and fouling up the banks so it was quiet once we were past the first lock. Jess walked along the narrow towpath behind me and said she'd choose the right spot. We passed the boat yard and St Barnabas church and the factory and then came to the quiet stretch where gardens run down to the water on one side and where a high brick wall skirts the towpath.

'Now!' Jess said.

I swung my arm and the bag arced through the air and splashed into the canal. Muddy rings spread out across the water and one bubble broke the surface. Ducks came excitedly to investigate.

·'That's finished,' I said, and turned to Jess. She was bringing a small camera down from her face.

'A little insurance,' she said, 'in case I need to write another anonymous letter.'

I stared at her, appalled. She had a photograph of me throwing a bag into the canal. Drag the canal and find the camera. Link me to the burglary. Who would believe my version? I wasn't sure I believed it myself.

I stepped towards her. Throw the camera in the canal and there would be no evidence. 'Stop there!' she said.

'Don't think I haven't planned everything, including your reaction. I'll tell you what I'll do. First, if you come any closer I'll scream. Boy attacks girl on towpath. You'll be the guilty one in everyone's eyes. Second, I'll throw the camera across into that garden. I've wound the film on so that even if the camera breaks open the film will probably be safe. The people there are friends of my parents so I'll be able to retrieve it. Why do you think I chose this exact spot?'

I didn't know how much to believe. If she screamed no one might hear. If she threw the camera in a hurry it might well fall in the water. She was probably lying about the garden; she wouldn't want the risk of being seen by people she knew, would she? The trouble was I didn't think I could risk it, now. Let her think she'd won and I might catch her off guard later.

'All right,' I said.

'Stay there,' she ordered. She opened the camera and took the film out and put it into her jeans' pocket. I could see the bulge against her thigh. There wasn't much chance of my taking her unawares.

She smiled at me. 'I do really want to be friends,' she said. 'It's just a bit of insurance.'

I turned round and walked on towards home. She walked behind, saying nothing for once. I brooded furiously in the silence. Did I want to be friends with her? Did she have another mad scheme that involved me? I didn't think I'd have much chance of saying no. Her file on me was rapidly fattening.

'I'll be in touch,' she said when we got to the next bridge. 'It may not be very soon. It's back to school on Monday and it'll be harder to escape. Dad blames me for the burglary, says if I hadn't broken the alarm the man wouldn't have got in. It was difficult enough getting out this morning. I had to spin big sister Anna some story. She's supposed to watch me when the parents aren't around. It's been fun. I'll see you, Dan.'

She walked over the bridge, waving at me without turning round. I walked on home, hoping that was it, that she'd forget me but half, no not half—a small part of me—hoped she would be in touch.

8

I didn't have long to wait. I had a letter sitting on the table when I came down to breakfast all ready for school on Monday. I knew Mum was even more curious than I was to see who it was from. I suppose I could, in theory, have left it until I was alone but that wasn't an option in practice.

I sliced the envelope neatly with my knife and pulled out the letter. A photograph fell out and Mum swooped on it like a rabid vulture. 'That's really good of you,' she said. 'Did your friend Jess take it?'

It was a good picture: bright, sharp, striking. I was swinging the Sainsbury's carrier bag at the end of my arm. You could almost see its trajectory over the plants on the bank and into the green water of the canal. My head was turned and you could see the surprise on my only too recognizable face.

'It's a funny picture,' Mum said. 'Very artistic. It looks as though you're about to throw something into the canal to get rid of it when someone spots you. It's like a scene from a film. You feel there's a real story behind it.' Her voice rose, as if she was asking a question, inviting a confidence.

'Just mucking about,' I said.

The letter was to the point:

Dear Dan
Here's a copy of the photo for your parents.
Hope they like it. I'm so pleased with it that
I've had several copies made.

Things are a bit busy here but I'll see you
next holidays—that's a promise.
Love,
Jess

Mum read the letter over my shoulder. 'What a nice girl,' she said. 'You'd better get off. You don't want to be late first day back.' As if I was ever allowed to be late!

The summons came on the first day of the next holidays, Saturday 7th April. Mum called up the stairs while I was trying to have a lie-in. 'You're to meet Jess at eleven at MOMA. I've ironed your best shirt. It's in the airing cupboard.'

'Hi!' Jess said. She was always there before me and always had a drink and a cake for me, and they were always different. I found this unnerving. 'Your mum told me how much she liked your photo.' She grinned, as if she'd done something very clever.

I sat down and glared at her. She laughed at me and in that moment I hated her. She must have realized she'd upset me because she stopped laughing and leant forward. 'I'm sorry, Dan. I just thought it would be better if as much as possible is out in the open. If most of what you say is true then people usually believe the bits that aren't.'

'I'm not used to telling lies,' I said, shirtily.

'Poor you,' Jess said.

'What do you want?'

'That's a bit ungracious,' she said. 'I've sent you a nice photo for your mum. I've bought you a drink and a slice of cake, and not a thank-you do I get, nor a "how are you and how did your term go?" You may be truthful but you're not very polite.'

I seethed with rage and nearly walked out.

'Sorry,' she said. 'You're not used to teasing, are you? You're an only, aren't you? Look, I didn't mean anything. It's just a joke. Enjoy your cake.'

I calmed myself down. I knew what she said was true. I had cousins who spent all their time teasing each other. I thought it was cruel but they seemed to cope. It made me look stuffy if I couldn't take it.

'Mum liked the photo,' I said. 'She said there was a story behind it.' Jess laughed, this time with me and not at me. 'And the cake's good,' I said. 'Thanks.'

'I've got a little job for you,' Jess said. I looked at her. I didn't like the sound of that at all. 'Don't worry,' she said, 'it's not our house again; it's another one.'

'Burglary?'

'That's right. You're so good it would be wrong to waste your talents.'

'I'm not doing any more burglary.'

Jess pulled a sheet of paper out of her pocket. 'This is the story that goes with the photograph. I've got lots of copies of this, too. It's not much of a story but it might interest a few people.' I read:

This photograph was taken on Thursday 22nd February by the canal behind number 31 Westmoor Road, North Oxford. It shows Daniel Gedding of 95 Meadow View Road, Lower Wolvercote, throwing a carrier bag into the canal. The bag contains a camera stolen from the house of Mr Andrew Arbour, 7 Frenchman's Road, on Tuesday 20th February.

'You'll be in trouble,' I said. 'Your film and my story should clinch it.'

'My film and the photographs and the copies of this are all well hidden, out of the house. Your story against mine? Do you want to try it?'

I didn't want to try it. I didn't want to find out if Mum and Dad would believe me at all. I didn't want to find out if they could forgive me for what I had done: the lies, the theft, the camera in the canal instead of at the menders. I didn't want interviews with the police. I didn't want newspaper reporters.

Jess sat grinning at me. I didn't want anything to do with her, either. The vague beginnings of an idea crept into my mind. I needed time to work it out. I needed to get back into her dad's study. I needed to be as cunning and two-faced as she was.

'What do you want me to do?'

'Nothing serious. Just a joke.'

She explained and I listened. She had a friend who lived in the next road. She was going away for two nights. Jess wanted to go into the house and totally rearrange her bedroom. Nothing was to be damaged, nothing taken. It wasn't a crime at all—just a joke, she said. When I said I didn't think it was very funny I had a long lecture on how sad people are who don't have a sense of humour. Eventually she let slip that she and her friend had had a long argument about somewhere they'd both been on holiday. Her friend had dared to say that Jess never noticed what was around her because she was too interested in herself. Jess said she was going to see her friend immediately they got back. 'I won't notice anything different in her room,' she said. 'That will really spook her. That will teach her.' I didn't dare say what I really thought.

'Breaking and entering's a crime,' I said.

She explained that there wouldn't be any breaking and entering. That was the whole point. Because this was Jess's best friend she knew the house well. She knew where there was a loo where she could take the bolt out of the window lock without anyone realizing. She knew the combination of the burglar alarm.

'Why me?'

It needed two people to move some of the furniture. Jess and her friend had done it once so she knew. There was absolutely nothing to worry about. The house would be empty. We would go in, switch off the burglar alarm, move everything according to the plan she had already made: furniture, contents of drawers and cupboards, posters, and so on. We would reset the burglar alarm and leave by the window. Jess would visit her friend the day they got back—she was her best friend so it would be the obvious thing for her to do—and replace the bolt.

Huge mystery. Big joke. No risk at all. I would tell my parents I was round at Jess's house. Her parents just needed to be spun some story.

Monday evening.

The plan that had been waking slowly in my brain sat up now. 'I've never officially been in your house, except the hall and under the first bed you come to,' I said. 'I'd better come before Monday to have my official look in case anyone asks me anything about it. Mum's very curious and's always asking questions: what colour are the curtains, that sort of thing.'

'Good chat-up line,' Jess said. 'Is that how you get in all the girls' bedrooms? Sorry, just teasing again. You're right. Do you want to come now? There'll be no one in there.'

She continued with jokes, what she thought were jokes, until we left the café. I was glad we both had our bikes because there was no way we could cycle side by side through the streets of Oxford so the journey was mercifully silent.

Once we were there she thought of a new joke. She gave me the grand tour, pretending to be a guide in some stately home, carefully describing every single curtain in the house and then testing me on what I had learnt as if I was at school. She even offered refreshments in the tea rooms afterwards. 'I'm sorry but our souvenir shop is currently closed,' she said.

It wasn't difficult to collect my own souvenir while she was making a drink. I slipped into her father's study and took his miniature tape recorder from the drawer and slipped it into my pocket. I needed to find out how to work it before I could put my plan into action.

We arranged to meet in the café on the day of the Big Joke, as Jess called it. I would be ready for her then.

9

My plan was simple. I would tape-record our planning meeting in the café and the tape would then be my Star Wars super-powerful deterrent against her weapons. I would make sure the conversation included enough damning references to the joy-riding and the burglary, and her entrapment of me. I would re-record the mini tape on to an ordinary cassette and give her the copy. I would buy a replacement tape and give it and the recorder to her to put back in her dad's drawer. I reckoned that would be enough to get her off my back. What particularly pleased me was the thought of beating her at her own game.

The plan was simple. I practised using the recorder. I taped it inside a plastic bag with holes in the bottom so that the microphone was opposite a hole. I practised switching it on by looking as if I was just moving the bag around, fiddling with it nervously. I worked out some leading remarks that would make Jess incriminate herself. I was very confident as I entered the café and sat down opposite her on Monday morning.

It worked perfectly. Jess had no suspicions at all. She said all the right things about joy-riding, burglary, and canals and was quite cutting about her parents. She detailed the evening's plans. I sat there totally confident. She had no idea that I was going to ring her up, play her selected extracts, and say goodbye.

I was over-confident. There was, of course, a fatal flaw. I had practised so much that the batteries were nearly exhausted and I had not thought about putting new ones in. When I played it back later, after taking batteries out of Mum's radio, I listened to me being polite to her about the walnut cake she had chosen, and then there was just my embarrassing stupid practising. Nothing useful, nothing incriminating, nothing I could play back to her without her falling off her chair laughing at me.

I could try again. I could buy new batteries. I could take the recorder with me tonight and go through with her mad scheme and then have a good recording.

I could bluff it. I could ring her and play the opening. She could call my bluff, demand a copy, demand to hear it all.

I bought new batteries.

The house was very like Jess's: detached, set back, with a shrubby front garden. There were two lights on, with open curtains. 'They're there!' I said, instinctively. Jess laughed. According to her, most people leave lights on time switches when they go away so that the house looks occupied and I remembered that her house had had lights on when I was breaking in there. She said that there definitely wasn't anyone in. She even took out her mobile and pressed some buttons. After a moment I heard the phone in the house ringing and ringing. No one answered it. She put it away and smiled.

'Don't panic,' she said. I found out that evening that breaking into someone else's house is less stressful if there are two of you, and that being given clear and sharp orders helps too. You just do what you're told and don't worry. If anyone caught us Jess had the front to talk her way out of trouble. I was almost enjoying myself. My main worry now was whether I was going to be able to get incriminating words on the tape recorder without her realizing what I was doing.

The road was quiet and, after a quick look up and down,

we walked through the gate as if we had every right to be there. She led the way down the side of the house and we were into darkness until a security light suddenly lit the side passage and us as though we were on stage.

'Down!' Jess said, and tugged my arm. I crouched, expecting windows to fly up and voices to bounce off me and police cars to screech to a halt, but absolutely nothing happened. Jess leant over and put her mouth to my ear: 'Cats set them off all the time,' she said, 'and a hedgehog does ours every night at ten o'clock.' We stood up. Bushes screened us from the road and a fence gave cover from next door. The light went off, leaving us blind in the dark.

Then we moved and it went on again and Jess swore. She led the way towards the back of the house. There was an outhouse, coal shed I guess, coming away from the main wall. 'There!' she said, and pointed to a small window with crinkled glass above it. I had been expecting something on the ground. Did she really expect me to climb up there in the full glare of the security light and clamber through that little window?

She didn't. She was going up. She told me exactly what she was going to do, probably to get her courage up. She was going to stand on the dustbin, pull herself on to the roof of the outhouse, lever the loo window open, climb through, run like mad down to the burglar alarm control box to type in the code before it went off.

She would then come and open the back door for me. She'd do the opposite when we'd finished. I had to stand there in the light and hammer like mad on the back door if anyone came.

Jess clambered on to the roof and strode confidently over the tiles. I cowered below, expecting to see her slip and roll to the ground shrieking in agony while all the neighbours rushed out of their houses. She opened the window and slid through. I found my hands going to my ears, anticipating the clamour of the alarm, but the suburban silence continued.

The back door opened. Jess beckoned me in. We were in a small entrance way, full of wellingtons and coats, and then through another doorway into a kitchen where surfaces and pans gleamed in the light that came through from the hall. Jess led me through, up the stairs and into a bedroom at the back. She went across to the window and closed the curtains and then came back and switched the light on. 'To work!' she said.

She was very efficient. She knew exactly where she wanted everything to go, and what order to move things in. We moved the furniture and then Jess started on the drawers. I said I wouldn't touch her friend's clothes and sat on the bed and watched. I wanted to take the tape recorder out but the light was bright and I had no disguise for it. I thought of putting it in my sleeve while Jess's back was turned but I caught her eye in the mirror. She smiled at me.

'Won't be long,' she said, and the doorbell rang.

'Shall I answer it?' I said, almost glad that we'd been caught and the whole nightmare was over.

'Shut up, idiot! Let's go and have a look.'

Jess went out across the hall and into a bedroom at the front that had no lights on. She walked to the side of the window and stood well back. I followed her and peered over her shoulder. There was nothing visible at all. I think I had expected to see the road full of police cars. The bell rang again, longer, more insistent. Jess's hand came back and gripped mine. It was the first sign of nervousness I had seen in her, or perhaps she was just making sure I didn't move.

After a long pause we saw a man walking away, down the path to the gate. Something about him worried me but I was pretty worried about the whole situation anyway. He went out and away down the road. 'Let's get finished and

46

out of here,' Jess said. She seemed flatter now, less real. She just tidied things up and then took her camera out and photographed the room and me in it before I realized what was happening. I didn't bother to complain. She had enough already; one more, a fairly harmless practical joke, wasn't going to make any difference.

I stood outside the back door while she reactivated the alarm and then came hastily and dishevelled out on to the roof. I had the recorder in my hand, hidden in my pocket, ready to bring out as soon as we were away from the glare of the security light. Jess dropped to the ground and we moved back into the safety of the bushes until the light went off.

I took the recorder out and pushed the switch. 'You've got me into some terrifying situations,' I said. 'Joy-riding Dad's car, blackmailing me into stealing your dad's camera, breaking into your friend's house—is that all now?' I waited for her reply to incriminate her so that I would be free from her for ever.

Her hand came over mine and eased the recorder out of my fingers. 'Nice try,' she said.

10

We came cautiously out of the gate. I was depressed at my total failure to get out of the mess I had been dragged into. Jess was flat. She'd obviously been hyped up this evening and was now having a reaction.

The road seemed empty and we were just stepping through the gate when we heard a car coming. In its headlights we saw that there was a man standing further down the road, the way we wanted to go, in the pool of darkness between lamp-posts. We stood in the gateway and Jess suddenly threw her arms around me. I stiffened and pulled away.

'Stand still, idiot,' she whispered into my ear. 'It's just camouflage. There's no need to get ideas. Pretend you're saying goodbye.'

'I wish I was.'

'I think it's the man who came to the house. What's he standing there for?'

I turned my head and looked down the road. The car had gone and it was difficult to see. Then the shape of the man went through the bright space under a light and away into the next patch of dark, a light, dark, and then round the corner into the main road. Jess released me and stood back. 'We may have saved them from a burglary,' she said. 'Our good deed for the day.'

We followed down towards the main road without speaking. The Woodstock Road was bright and busy with traffic. Standing on the kerb at the pelican lights, waiting to cross, was the man. He turned and I suddenly knew who he was and where I had seen him. He had been halfway up the stairs in Jess's house with a look of surprise on his face. He had the same look of surprise now.

The lights turned red and the traffic stopped. The crossing beeped and the green man shone but my man stepped towards me. A car blew its horn and a young man leant out of the driver's window and shouted something rude. The man ignored him and came on towards me.

The red light changed to flashing amber and I came to my senses and shouted to Jess, 'That's the man!' and turned and ran back the way we had come. 'Dan!' Jess shouted.

There was no sound of pursuit. I looked over my shoulder. Nothing. I stopped running and struggled to control my breathing. Still nobody came round the corner, not the man, not Jess.

I knew I had to go back. Whatever Jess had done to me, I had to go back. I had this picture in my mind of Jess being dragged across the road flailing feebly, the man's hand over her mouth stopping her from crying out. I didn't have a picture of me rushing up and beating him off, but I had to go back.

I walked round the corner. The pavement was empty. I ran back to the crossing, looking wildly round. A few cars passed, intent on their "urgent voluntary errands"—a phrase from a poem we'd read in school came stupidly into my mind. A white van pulled away from the kerb in the side road opposite.

Jess was in it! She had been dragged to the van, thrown in the back, and was being driven away. The number! I had to get the van's number! 'Jess!' I screamed.

I ran straight across the road. There was a screeching of brakes and a car's horn blaring. A man shouted at me from the car but I ran on, not looking back. I had to get the number of the van.

It drove round the bend in the road before I could read it. I stopped, panting. There was no point in going on now. I had to go back to Jess's house and tell her parents some story, let the adults take over, and just hope too much didn't come out about what we'd been up to. Such trouble she'd got me into.

I walked back to the main road, dreading what I had to do. Even though there weren't any cars coming I pressed the button for the crossing lights and waited for the green man. I was beginning to realize how nearly I'd been hit by that car, how nearly hit, thrown in the air to smash lifeless on the tarmac. I started trembling.

'Sir Lancelot the perfect knight,' came Jess's voice. I was so shaken by what had happened that I thought I was hallucinating. Then she stepped out of the front garden of the house next to the crossing and came up and hugged me. I was so out of it that I let her for a moment, and almost enjoyed it. The house behind her had lights on behind carefully drawn curtains and ignored us politely, or indifferently.

I pulled away from her. 'What happened?' I asked.

'I shouted for you and then I ran into the garden and hid in the bushes down the side passage. I heard the row in the road and came to look. You were pretty impressive.'

'I thought he'd got you,' I said. 'I really didn't want to have to tell anyone what had been going on. I just panicked, didn't stop to think.'

'I owe you,' she said.

'You'll give me the photos?'

She laughed. 'Give me a couple of days to get these developed. Meet me on Wednesday, usual time, usual place. Bye!' She was gone, running off down the road.

I started walking home. I found I was almost sorry it was all over. It had been terrifying at times, almost all the time, but it was addictive. Being normal, sensible, predictable was pretty boring. Jess was exciting. I told myself I'd been unbelievably lucky not to be caught. All the way home I ran alternative endings through my mind: being caught by the burglar, being caught by the owners of the house, being caught by Neighbourhood Watch, the police . . . I managed to frighten myself into being glad it was finished. On Wednesday I'd have the photos. They'd be a good souvenir.

I was first at the café on Wednesday. This was so unusual that I thought it must be one of Jess's jokes: leave me sitting there looking stupid and embarrassed until I finally got up and stumbled out to the amused smiles of the other customers. I wasn't falling for that. I turned and walked out. But suppose she was just late, had been held up somehow?

I went up the steps to the little museum book shop. I could stay here, browsing among the books and postcards, and could keep watch out of the window at the same time.

I didn't have long to wait. I saw Jess running past the window and into the entrance. I put down the book of photographs I'd been looking at and went after her. I stood for a moment just inside the door and watched her. She was twitching in the queue. She was acting 'nervous' like you might in a drama lesson, almost overacting it, constantly looking round, fidgeting in sharp and jerky movements.

She saw me and beckoned, almost surreptitiously. 'What do you want?' she said. She was behaving so out of character that at first I didn't realize she was talking about drinks and cakes. She paid. I realized that she always paid and then I thought that I wasn't there by choice, and that her family was obviously much better off than mine so I let my money slide back down my pocket and followed her to the table she had chosen. This wasn't her usual one at which she could see and be seen by everyone but was in the dark corner, opposite the door.

'What's up?' I said.

She started crying, which was another first, and one I could have done without. I was finding this difficult to cope with. What was I supposed to do: ignore it politely, pass her a neatly ironed white handkerchief, draw her weeping face to my manly chest? I ate a piece of cake.

She picked up the paper serviette from the tray and blew her nose. 'Sorry,' she said. She took a sip of her coffee and then said, 'He was waiting outside my house.'

I stared at her. 'The man?' She nodded. Of course the man knew her house. He might not know she lived there. He probably thought I did. I was the one he'd seen. I was the one who knew he was a burglar, who could identify him.

'I'm the one he's after,' I said.

11

J ess stared at me. 'If he's after you, why's he watching my house?'

For a moment I felt superior. She had always, up to now, been several steps ahead of me, and had enjoyed taunting me with my slowness. I spoke slowly, as if to a small child. 'He thinks I live there. He saw me in the house when he broke in.'

She sagged with relief. 'That's all right then. It was a nasty moment, though. I had to make a daring escape.' She started on an account that could have come straight off some TV story.

She didn't know how long the man had been watching her house, she told me. Her road, like every road in Oxford, every road in the whole country, is always full of parked cars, skips, and builders' vans and so one white van more or less wouldn't attract her attention. Yesterday afternoon when she'd come back from collecting her photos from Boots she'd happened to notice a van with a man inside reading a newspaper. That wasn't unusual either.

She started to get worried when she looked out of her bedroom window and saw the van was still there and the man was still sitting inside it. White vans are common enough but after the previous night one behaving strangely was a danger sign. Next time she looked the van was gone and she tried to persuade herself that it had been a nothing.

In the morning she looked out and could see no sign of him so she went off to do her paper round. 'Paper round?' I said, but she ignored me. Innocent-looking cars lined the kerb and she felt a sudden relief. It had worried her more than she had realized. When she came home she spotted it, further down the road. The reflected light off its windscreen stopped her seeing if there was anyone in it, but she was convinced it was the same van in a different parking slot.

She had to get out to meet me. She thought up various plans, like climbing over the back wall and going through the garden behind but in the end decided that on her bike she should be able to out-pedal the man if he followed her on foot, and lose him round one way streets if he followed in his van. If she was lucky, if she went the other way down the road, he might not even realize she'd gone.

As she sat opposite me in the café telling me this I could see that she was still jittery. I had thought she was quite fearless, would do anything. This man had rattled her badly, as he had me, and I began to feel just a little sympathy for her. I still thought she was braver than me; she was here, after all. I would still be in the house.

Her flying exit was nearly a disaster. She had poised herself ready to screech out of her gateway, had tensed her foot on the pedal, had taken in a deep breath, when she heard voices coming towards her. Two women were dawdling along the pavement. She had so nearly ridden straight into them, bringing the three of them crashing to the pavement. The man would have rushed over to help and somehow got her into his van, perhaps by pretending to take her to hospital.

She waited until they had gone past and then shot out after them, ringing her bell like mad, hands on the brakes just in case. Luckily they turned and dithered enough for her to squeeze through, apologizing profusely. They were not happy.

She managed to miss an old man on the corner, cycled along the pavement and turned down the next side road and stopped in a gateway. No white van screeched down the road after her. She decided to leave her bike there and take a bus down to Oxford. She didn't like the idea of cycling along worrying about someone driving up behind her and nudging her off her bike. She was lucky. A bus was coming along as she went up to the main road. She waved at the driver and managed to cross. As the bus drove along she kept looking back but there was still no white van.

'That's why I'm late,' she said. 'And I've still got to get home. And there'll be other days. I can't cope with this, Dan.'

'Awful,' I said, and took a bite out of my cake. It was her fault she was in this mess, entirely her fault. And what was I supposed to do about it? I was a bit ashamed to find that I was almost glad she was on the receiving end for a change. 'Awful,' I said again and then realized this sounded just wet and thought I ought to say something a bit more positive.

'Did you get the number of the van?'

She said I might as well ask if she'd recited the whole of 'The Lady of Shalott' while hanging upside down from a lamp-post and juggling three goldfish bowls, complete with goldfish. I plainly had no idea, no idea at all, of the stress she had been under. No doubt some sort of superman like me would have calmly taken out a notebook and pencil and written down the number but she was just concerned with getting away alive, and if I didn't have anything constructive to say I might as well shut up.

Which I did.

I looked at the exhibition that was hanging on the walls of the café. At first I just thought they were pictures behind glass but I suddenly realized that mirrors were hanging round the three walls (the serving counter made up the fourth wall). The mirrors had somehow been painted on so that only patches reflected. If I got my head in the right position I could see one picture reflected in another. I stood up and managed to get three reflecting together. I've always loved that feeling of falling into infinity you get if you line mirrors up carefully.

'What on earth are you doing?'

'It's all done with mirrors,' I said without thinking, and sat down.

'Sometimes I wonder if you're all there,' Jess said sharply.

I'd had enough of her. She had caused me so much trouble and upset, had got herself into real trouble, and was now taking it out on me. I certainly wasn't all there for her; I didn't want to be there at all, though I'd quite like a better look at the mirror pictures—and the cake was good. I certainly wasn't having her sitting there insulting me. The way to show I wasn't daft was to make my remark make sense.

'It's very simple,' I said, speaking slowly and patiently again. It was a childish way of getting my own back but I enjoyed it. I held up my hand and ticked points off on my fingers. 'You don't want to go to the police. You don't want to tell your parents. The man is bigger and stronger than you so you can't beat him up. You can't have plastic surgery, change your name, and live abroad for the rest of your life.'

She was beginning to seethe with irritation and I waggled my thumb at her. 'The only thing left,' I said, 'is what I suggested and what you sneered at.' I paused, waggling my thumb irritatingly as long as I dared. 'Trickery,' I said, putting my finger on to my thumb. 'All done with mirrors, as I said.'

'I'm sorry,' Jess said. 'I was wrong. Perhaps you're not quite as daft as you look. So, what's your great plan?'

'I haven't worked out all the details yet,' I said, which wasn't entirely true. I hadn't worked out any details at all.

'Pencil and paper,' Jess said. 'Hang on!' She went off out of the café and came back a few minutes later with a notebook and pencil she'd bought in the book shop above. She'd brightened up and was taking charge again.

'Right, what do we know?' she said.

'What does *he* know?' I said, a bit narked that she was taking over my idea, forgetting I didn't actually have an idea at all.

'That's right,' she said, giving me a big smile, one that was too obviously meant to make me feel better, but which, irritatingly, did. She wrote the heading: *WHAT MAN KNOWS*.

12

It was funny, really. All we had written down was:

> *he knew where ~~I live Jess~~ one of us lives*
> *that Dan recognized him*
> *and was scared of him*

We argued over 'scared', but that was it.

'You're the face in the mirror,' Jess said suddenly. I thought she'd flipped. 'Don't you see? He knows nothing about you. I bet he thinks he does. He thinks you live in my house. In fact, he was probably following me to find out where I live. He's got it back to front.' She scribbled down:

> **WHAT THE MAN <u>THINKS</u> HE KNOWS**
> *where Dan lives*
> *that Dan and I are friends*

'Why doesn't he think we're brother and sister?' I asked.

'He's only seen us together once, and only out of the house. You were in my house when he burgled it, and I left the house by myself. Anyway, we don't look a bit alike, and anyone can see you fancy me.'

I stared at her. How could she say things like that? I certainly didn't fancy her; she was nothing but trouble. You might as well say that a rabbit frozen in the headlights fancies the car that's about to run it over.

'The point is,' she said, 'we know more than he does because we know where he's wrong.'

We rambled round and round this for ages, getting nowhere. We argued about who the man thought lived where. I said he'd seen her coming and going at her house too often but she was determined to believe that he didn't know where she lived. I realized that the thought spooked her and in the end shut up and didn't argue any more.

'What's this paper round?' I asked.

'I need the money,' she said.

Her father had blamed her—it was so unfair, she said, at some length—for the burglary. He reckoned that if she hadn't fiddled with the alarm system it wouldn't have happened. He stopped her pocket money to pay for the repairs. She wasn't allowed to do a paper round because this would make the punishment less, so she pretended she was going to the early morning training session at the Ferry Centre swimming pool. She wrapped a towel round her head before she came in. She had forged her father's signature on the consent form.

'No one bothers about me really anyway,' she said. 'They're always on about what I'm doing and where I'm going and when I've got to be in by but they aren't interested in me as a person. If they were, they wouldn't do this to me.' She was now worried about getting in and out to do her paper round without the man jumping her. She wanted me to turn up every morning and escort her. I said I wouldn't be allowed and she got abusive. Things got rather tense.

Jess still thought I'd worked out some brilliant master plan and wouldn't tell her because I was sulking. I was sulking because she'd said I fancied her and I was determined to prove I didn't even like her. In the end she persuaded me that it was worth making him go on thinking that was where I lived. She had some idea about setting a trap for him, mad schemes in which he was lured into what he thought was a house empty but for me, the bait.

In the end I weakly agreed to come back to her house and look as if I was coming in but not going out, while she got back in without him seeing her. I continued a mild sulk but it wasn't too difficult to keep it up as we walked back along the canal towpath. She was pushing her bike and there wasn't room for us to walk side by side so I could trail gloomily behind her.

When we came to the bridge near her road we stopped and she explained again exactly what I had to do. She got on her bike and cycled off. I was suddenly frightened. I had to walk on my own up the road, looking totally unconcerned, and into the driveway of a house that wasn't mine, a house I'd recently been terrified in.

I turned and started on along the towpath towards home. Then I stopped. I heard Jess's voice clearly in my head accusing me of being too cowardly to do what she had already done. Going home wasn't a solution. She wouldn't just leave me alone. I wasn't yet out of her power.

Reluctantly I left the safety of the canal and walked up the road. Madness, I said to myself, madness, madness. I struggled not to keep turning my head; Jess had stressed that the man mustn't know that I thought the house was being watched. I'd said that this was silly; if we were such friends she'd have rung me up and told me. 'Not if you're out,' she'd replied. And then she'd said it was a mistake to think other people always work everything out. And then: 'Just do it, Dan.'

I was doing it. I was walking up the pavement as if I was coming home free of care. I was on the opposite pavement to Jess's house. She'd said this gave me more flexibility. She had painted an unnervingly convincing picture of me coming past the van. As I came level the man threw his door open, knocking me to the ground. He leapt out, picked me up while I was still stunned, threw me into the back of the van, and drove screeching off. If I was on the wrong pavement I could innocently cross the road where I wanted.

There was no white van between me and the house, just tightly parked cars in various colours. I began to hope that the man wasn't there at all. Why should he be? If we were going to the police, surely we'd have gone by now? I suddenly wondered if Jess was actually making this all up. She'd seemed pretty upset, but she was a practised liar. No burglar in his right senses would lurk outside a house where he had been seen by one of the family. This was an elaborate practical joke.

I nearly, so nearly, turned round and went home. I didn't because I was angry that she'd taken me in and made a fool of me. She'd turned up with this ludicrous story and so convinced me it was true that I was walking up her road in a state of terror while she was probably looking out of an upstairs window and laughing at me. Go home, my common sense said. Get your own back, my anger said.

I slowed my already slow pace. My mind accelerated away with its new scenario. I suddenly start running, skitter across the road, and tear into her front gate, rush through to the back and find somewhere to hide. She's watching and isn't sure what's going on. Has she so convinced my cowardly mind that I see imaginary burglars leaping out of white vans all along the road? Is there, could there possibly be, something real happening? Was I, perhaps, just pretending to believe her and am now mocking her lies?

She comes out to find me. I ignore her call and remain hidden, watching as she looks for me, her uncertainty and anxiety increasing. When she finds me I pull her down so that she too is hidden and I tremble out the terrible news . . .

I couldn't do it. Reluctantly I walked across the road and down the front drive of her house. Jess had told me to go to the side door so that I wouldn't be seen ringing the front door bell of what was supposed to be my own home. Just as I got there Jess's older sister came out. I remembered her from the burglary, and by the way she looked at me I knew she remembered me too. She had that self-confidence that makes me curl up inside but otherwise looked just like an older Jess.

'Yes?' she said, and stared at me.

'I'm . . . er . . . looking for Jess.'

'Have you tried the front door bell?' she asked, as if she knew perfectly well that I hadn't.

'Hi, Dan!' Jess called, coming up the back garden. Her sister turned and gave her a withering look.

'Do try to train your friends to use the front door,' she said. 'Some of them might even be bright enough to learn how to press a door bell, if you're really patient with them. Though I suppose that if they're stupid enough to be friends of yours they must be beyond hope.' She went back into the house.

'Ignore her,' Jess said. 'My big sister Anna. She's impossible. And she's joined the enemy; spends all her time spying on me for the parents. How did you get on?'

'There's no white van out there,' I said. I nearly said that I didn't believe there had ever been, but I thought I'd keep that to myself for the moment.

Jess said we should continue with the plan just in case the man was watching from somewhere else or from a car we didn't know about. She led me down the garden to the wall at the bottom. She pushed a wheelbarrow up to the corner.

'There's a compost heap on the other side to break the drop,' she said. 'Just go straight through the garden. I think they're out. I'll stand on the barrow and watch you till you get to the road. If anyone says anything, just leave them to me.'

I climbed into the barrow, which tipped alarmingly. Jess clucked and held the handles to steady it. I pulled myself on to the wall. Not far below me was the compost pile, covered with an old shower curtain. The garden stretched down to the house and I could just glimpse the road beyond. I turned back to say goodbye to Jess and saw her sister staring at me from an upstairs window.

I dropped down and walked away. I was not coming back to be the family joke.

No one challenged me as I walked through their garden and past the house. Instinctively I turned to look at the house number, just in case. I turned to go home and found myself staring at the man.

13

I turned and ran back through the garden, up on to the compost heap, and scrambled over the wall. The wheelbarrow tipped under my feet and I fell sprawling on the ground. The windows of the house stared blankly at me as I limped out. I could see no one in the road when I looked out of the gate, so I turned towards the canal and went home

'Your friend Jess rang,' Mum said when I got home. 'She was sorry to have missed you.' Since Jess knew perfectly well I would be out, I thought that was a bit unlikely and just grunted.

'Don't you want to know what she said?' Mum asked, with the suggestive leer she always had when she, increasingly often, referred to Jess. The honest answer was, no I certainly did not want to hear, but I couldn't say that, so I grunted again.

It seemed that Jess had persuaded Mum that an early morning swimming session was just what I needed and I was to meet her outside her house at seven fifteen sharp. 'Sharp,' Mum repeated as if this was some wonderful piece of news to be savoured. I stared at her. Jess knew how to get her own way all right, the scheming, conniving, spoilt little . . .

There was no question of my conveniently oversleeping in the morning. Mum had me up with a cup of tea and a piece of toast. She said I couldn't go out with nothing but I couldn't have a proper breakfast until I got home. She had been all for driving me round but I insisted on going on my bike. If she'd taken me she'd have wanted to sit and watch this imaginary training session.

I was tempted to lurk about the towpath until it was time to go home again, but I was sure that if I didn't turn up at seven fifteen sharp Jess would be back on the phone to Mum. I cycled warily up her road but there weren't any white vans parked and there was no one lurking about, except Jess inside her front gate. We collected her bag of papers from the newsagent and set off to deliver them. At first Jess made me act as look-out, standing on the pavement and swivelling my head a hundred and eighty degrees every few seconds, but it was soon obvious that we hadn't been followed and there was so little chance of the man just happening to come along that she let me deliver some of the papers.

The last lot of papers was for the big block of retirement flats on the corner of the main road. Jess typed in a code on the entry phone, the door buzzed and we went in. It was eerily silent and smelt of polish inside the entry hall. Jess pressed the button for the lift and we went up to the top floor. She went down the corridor to stick newspapers through letter boxes and I looked out of the windows. The front one gave a view over tree tops into Oxford with spires scratching the sky and the rush hour beginning to build up on the main road.

I crossed the landing to the window at the back. This looked over roof tops and gardens. Straight below was the car park for the block. Parked innocently at the end of a row was a familiar-looking white van. I stood and stared at it.

'Come on,' Jess said, 'next floor down.'

'Look at this,' I said. She stood next to me and stared down.

'There's no one in it,' she said.

'The world's full of white vans,' I said.

65

'But not with blue sponges on the dashboard on the passenger side,' she said.

I looked down. There was something blue inside the van but I couldn't see what it was from here. 'I saw it when the van was after me,' Jess said. 'I'm sure its the same one. But the man didn't look old enough to be living here, not by years and years.'

'He could be working here.'

We walked down the stairs to the next floor. Somehow the lift now looked like a trap. One of the flat doors was open and an old lady leapt out on Jess as if her arrival was the high-spot of her day. How was she? What sort of day was it out there? Wasn't the news terrible? Who's your friend? I hope you're not going to give us up; it's so nice having a trustworthy girl. No offence, young man, but we do feel safer with a girl. I laughed inside at the thought of anyone feeling safe with Jess around.

'Is that your white van down in the car park, Mrs Fawley?' Jess asked when there was the briefest pause in the flow. Mrs Fawley obviously thought this was the best joke she'd heard for days but eventually told us that the van belonged to the very nice young Mr Grafton, the caretaker who looked after them so well.

Jess interrogated Mrs Fawley brilliantly, not that she was unwilling to talk, just careful steering the way we wanted her to go. Eventually we got away and finished the papers, more nervous now that we knew we were in the enemy's own territory. I saw Jess back to her gate and she thanked me profusely for coming with her as she wrapped her towel round her head. 'Eleven at MOMA,' she said, and left me to go home and face all Mum's questions.

Things seemed to be back to normal when we met. Jess was at her favourite table with a cappuccino and a slice of fudge cake waiting for me, my share of the paper round she said. She had written down what we'd learnt from Mrs Fawley and went through it for me.

Steve Grafton had a small flat on the ground floor at the back of the block. He did the maintenance for the flats and the cleaning of the public areas like staircases. He was always willing to put himself out, especially when the residents had trouble with their electricals. He'd programme their videos, mend their TVs. When they couldn't be mended he'd get them replacements, good-as-new second hand at very reasonable prices. Almost anything they wanted, he seemed to know where to get a bargain. He'd even get things for their friends who didn't live there. He couldn't be more helpful. And he sold them fresh organic vegetables from his allotment. A much valued man, he was.

'Designer burglary,' Jess said. 'A neat little scheme.' She took an envelope out of her pocket and passed it over to me. 'Mr Stephen Grafton' was typed on the outside. 'Open it,' Jess said. Inside was a letter. It had today's date on the top but no address.

Steve,
We know that you have been burgling houses and selling TVs, videos, etc. to some of us in the retirement flats. We also know that you have been following children around. This must stop at once or we will send our file to the police.
You will hear from us again.

I folded the letter and put it back in the envelope. I wasn't sure what to think. Wouldn't this just make him more determined to get us? Jess dismissed my worries.

'Can't you see that he'll think it doesn't actually come from us but from one of the oldies? That's what's so clever about it. At the moment he's just worried about us, who we might tell, so he wants to silence us. Now he'll think that silencing us will just make things worse.'

'If he believes the letter. How many of those oldies have a computer? He'll surely know and that will narrow the suspects down. You could be putting some total innocent in danger.'

'I'm a total innocent and I'm in danger,' Jess said. I just looked at her. She seemed to believe it.

'Suppose not one of them has a computer,' I said.

'All right. I'll write it out in a disguised oldie-looking handwriting,' she said. 'Will that satisfy you? Or have you got some better idea?'

As I had no ideas at all we agreed that she would write it out and post it through the flat's letter box that afternoon, if the coast was clear. She was going to the newsagent's to see if she could change her round but she wanted me on escort duty at seven fifteen sharp again.

'I can't,' I said. 'We're going to my gran's. We always leave early, about seven. Ring Mum and ask her if you don't believe me, you two get on so well. And thanks for the cake.'

I left. It may have been a small victory, but it was one. I really didn't think she'd ring to check.

14

That small victory seemed to keep Jess away for a long time. School wasn't so bad now. I had a secret life the others knew nothing about and somehow it gave me invisible armour. I couldn't forget her though, not least because she sent me picture postcards regularly and always managed to include a message I'd understand but that Mum wouldn't. Between the two of them I knew I hadn't escaped, yet.

At the beginning of the summer holidays Jess summoned me for coffee and cake. She greeted me as if we'd seen each other the day before and passed me the previous day's *Oxford Mail*, folded to an inside page where she had circled an item in red.

Teen 'Tecs to Test Tobacconists

A special squad of under-age 'smokers' is to be recruited to catch tobacconists and newsagents who are selling cigarettes to children. With increasing numbers of school children starting smoking there is to be a major campaign to enforce the law. The snooper squad will be specially trained and will be under constant adult observation while they attempt to buy cigarettes.

There was more about penalties and safeguards, and quotations from various people who were for or against the scheme.

I looked at her. 'Are you thinking of applying?'

'We're setting up our own squad,' she said. 'Do stop bleating and just listen.'

Her plan was very simple. We would go into shops and try to buy cigarettes. If we were sold any we would take out the mini cassette player I had tried to use on her back in April, produce the newspaper article, and ask for a hundred pounds for our silence.

Her reasons were very simple, so simple that really she shouldn't have to spell them out even to someone as gormless as me. She had given up her paper round the day I 'let her down' as she had been scared of the man grabbing her. Anyway it was just too boring. (Too much like work for a spoilt rich kid, I thought, but I kept my mouth shut.) She had had her pocket money, 'allowance' she called it now, stopped again though she wouldn't say why. She had thought of starting a paper round again and getting me to accompany her on her round as her minder, but this scheme was better. She didn't have a lot of time before they were off to Italy.

And no, I didn't actually have any choice. Her dossier on me was bulging and she wouldn't hesitate to use it. She put it all clearly and simply, as if talking to a rather stupid child. Perhaps this was when the worm should have turned. I should never have been a worm at all, should have called her bluff that very first time. Each time you give in to bullies it gets harder and harder to stand up to them next time. Still, this was different. This was serious.

I did try. I said that what we were doing was criminal: extorting money with menaces, blackmail. She started on about Robin Hood. 'No decent person will sell us cigarettes,' she said. 'That will be the end of the story for them. If anyone sells cigarettes to us they're criminals and deserve what they get. They won't dare to go to the police. We'll have the evidence of their crime on tape, and we certainly

70

won't be recording what happens next. It'll teach them a lesson. We'll be doing a public service: protecting the health of children and saving the courts all the cost of a trial. And if there's any trouble, we just run for it. We'll suss out our escape route first.'

Next morning the worm was standing with Jess outside a newsagent's well away from where either of us lived. I was feeling quite cheerful because we had been refused cigarettes four times already, and mainly by rather rude shopkeepers. I didn't enjoy being told off but it was much better than what Jess had planned. I'd already suggested that we should give up, that they'd all been warned by the article in the paper about a crack-down, but she wouldn't listen.

This was a depressing shop in a depressing area. It was in a row of four shops but the other three were all boarded up and covered with graffiti. This one's dirty windows and door had bars across so that you had to lean right up to the glass to peer in. Jess pushed the door and an electric bell rang shrilly. She kept a firm grip on my arm and dragged me behind her into the shop. I expected to see a sad little old man in slippers hunched up behind the counter but even in the gloom inside this hopeless place I could see that there was no one there. We could grab a packet and run, I thought, and then realized that wasn't the point.

The door behind the counter opened. The room behind was brightly lit and I could only see the silhouette of a powerfully-built man. 'Yes?' he said.

Jess nudged me, but I said nothing. We'd had an agreement, which meant as always that she'd told me what I was going to agree with, that she would ask men and I'd ask women. She said you always got a better reception from the opposite sex. Eventually she said, 'Twenty cigarettes, please, the cheapest.' The man stood there, black against the light. After a long pause he stretched out his arm and slapped the counter.

'Out!' he said.

'Please. Just ten would do, please?'

'Out before I throw you out.'

I tugged at Jess and we backed out. The silhouette stared at us until we were out of the shop. Our bikes were round the corner but Jess just stood by hers. She took out her tape recorder and rewound the tape without playing it.

'It's hopeless,' I said. 'There's been too much publicity. If we've seen the newspaper you can be sure the newsagents have. They sell the paper, and they'll warn each other. No one's going to sell to kids at the moment. It was a great idea but give it a few months,' I rambled on. There was no way I'd have anything to do with Jess in a few months. I needed to find some way of getting free from her, and an idea was beginning to surface in my mind.

'Do stop wittering on, Dan,' she said. 'There's something fishy going on here.' I didn't point out that what was fishy was her elaborate mad schemes; she didn't seem in the mood for the truth. 'Come on!'

She walked off down the side road and turned right into an alley that turned a right-angle and ran behind the shops. Dustbins and litter were the only things I could see but she seemed fascinated. She turned and walked back to our bikes. 'I knew it was fishy,' she said. I had no idea what she was on about. In fact I just thought she was spinning stories to bluster her way out of a humiliation. Keeping quiet was my best policy, keeping quiet and working out how to get out of this whole stupid situation. I should have known that the one thing Jess couldn't cope with was being ignored. She'd said once that she got enough of that at home and she certainly wasn't going to put up with it from me.

'Didn't you see?' I shook my head. All I'd seen was what I expected: town grot. 'That shop and the one next to it have got identical bars on the windows, all the windows.'

'So what?' I said. I really couldn't see what she was getting at.

'Sometimes, Daniel, you are so stupid. Just think, for once. Why has an empty shop got bars on all its windows? Why are they identical to the ones next door?'

'Simple,' I said, irritated by her even more than usual. 'The empty shop used not to be empty. They spent so much on fancy bars that they went bankrupt. The shop that's still open got them done at a discount, like double-glazing firms offer. You know, be the first in your neighbourhood, have an advertising board outside, and we'll do you cheaply. So they haven't gone bust quite yet.'

If I thought she'd be impressed by my nice simple explanation I was wrong. All she said was that I obviously needed a fix of coffee. We cycled back to the Museum of Modern Art and she bought me a cappuccino and a piece of lemon cake. She then told me exactly what I should have seen and worked out. It was like Sherlock Holmes deducing from a dusty hat that a man was unhappily married because his wife didn't bother to brush it before he went out. Suppose she had, I always wanted to ask Holmes, but he had walked through a building site on the way and got it dusty again? Watson never asked the sensible questions. He just sat there with his mouth open, believing everything he was told.

If I'd learnt from Watson I'd have been more sensible.

Jess said that the bars had obviously been put up after the shop had closed. The shop was being used to store something valuable. The valuables were illegal or they wouldn't be hidden in this disguised way. The man in the open shop couldn't make a living out of what his shop sold, and he was too keen to get rid of us and too fly to give anything away. We had stumbled on a sure-fire money spinner. We had to go back and keep it under observation but we needed a cover story.

'School project,' I said without thinking, and kicked myself.

That was, apparently, the first sensible thing I'd ever said. Kids with clipboards are doing a school project and are harmless.

Jess? Harmless?

15

I decided I'd be a planner when I grew up—if I grew up. With Jess around that seemed increasingly unlikely. I actually found myself enjoying working out our bogus school project. If school ever allowed us to work anything out for ourselves I might even enjoy that too. Jess just wanted to get back to the shop and wasn't interested but I said it was essential that the project sounded convincing.

We'd been into Ryman's on our way down High Street and she'd bought a clipboard. A sudden meanness had come over her and she refused to buy one each, said that a board and pen and pad of paper was quite enough to pay for when we hadn't yet got anything back from any of the tobacconists. She said our survey had to be about shopping because that way we could ask questions about 'our' shop without anyone getting suspicious. She seemed to think that was enough planning; that we'd just go out, stop people, and ask them if they ever went in that shop. When I suggested that it didn't sound a very convincing school project she pushed the clipboard over to me. I opened the pad and started making notes. I dragged up memories of boring geography lessons and decided that five questions was about right. I enjoyed working out exactly what to ask and was looking forward to trying the questionnaire out.

Jess wasn't impressed, and was less impressed when I said we ought to start somewhere away from the shop. I said it would give us time to get into the act, to be convincing. She said it would be a waste of time and that I was a coward looking for any excuse to avoid going back.

I should have said that only idiots walked into real and serious danger with their eyes open, but I didn't. I was too cowardly. She sat opposite me with her eyebrows raised, sneering, and I weakly gave in and followed her out and cycled after her back to the road with those menacing shops.

Here the flaw in the survey became obvious. There was no one in the road. While I had been planning the questions I had pictured something like the corner shop at home with people around: going to the shop, getting off the bus, walking their dogs on to Port Meadow—normal life.

A white van came out of the side road to the corner where we were standing. It braked suddenly. The lorry behind hooted angrily and the van accelerated away. 'Was that him?' Jess asked.

'Who?'

'Your burglar in the white van who was after me. You know, Steve, Steve . . . Steve Grafton.'

'I don't know,' I said, irritably. I was worried enough about what we were doing now without having anything else added on. 'I couldn't see the driver. Anyway, it's gone now.'

Jess was peering down the road. 'Is he turning back?' she said. I couldn't see anything except the lorry that had hooted and I just didn't want to think about white vans. The best thing was for us to move away.

'We can't stand here,' I said. 'No one would stand here doing a survey. We're obviously up to something.'

'I knew your survey was rubbish,' Jess said. 'Give me the board.'

She turned to a clean sheet of the pad and wrote 'CHANGE OF BUILDING USE' across the top. 'Name of street?'

'Blakeney Road,' I said, and watched her write it down and underline it. She wrote numbers down the page in the margin and at the bottom wrote 'KEY' and a ✓. We locked our bikes and walked along the road. Jess passed the first two houses and put a tick on her list and stopped at the third. 'Look!' she said, pointing at the door. 'Four doorbells. Change from family house to bedsits. House number?'

'Five,' I said sulkily. She could see the number on the door as well as I could. She scribbled on the pad and then moved on. One house she said was occupied by students as the front garden was a total mess and full of black bin bags. We carefully didn't look at the shops on the other side of the road as we passed them but kept on slowly. Near the corner we saw a woman coming towards us and Jess passed me the clipboard.

'Carry out your survey,' she said.

'Excuse me,' I said. The woman wouldn't stop, just said she was busy, and walked on. Jess laughed and took the clipboard back from me. We crossed the road and started back towards the shops. A van came down the road towards us. The driver slowed as he came up to the shops, tooted his horn briefly, drove past, and then reversed into the alley.

'Gotcha!' Jess said. 'What's its number?'

I didn't know. All I knew was that a medium-sized ordinary-looking blue van had arrived. It seemed a good time for us to go. Jess, of course, didn't agree.

'Come on!' she said. 'We've got a survey to finish for school.'

We walked along towards the shops, passing houses that were still just houses and so needed only a tick. Her sheet was beginning to look almost real, which may be why I tagged along behind her, almost believing we were doing something sensible.

We came to the alleyway along the side of the shops. Jess sketched on her pad: a row of four shops, the first she wrote 'empty' on, the second 'bars', the third 'newsagent', and the fourth 'empty'. 'We'd better take a look down here,' Jess said brightly and quite loudly. 'We must do the survey properly.' She strode down to where the alley turned at the back of the shops and stopped. I lagged behind her, knowing this wasn't a good idea. Just before the corner was a clutter of dustbins and wheelie bins. The van sat just round the corner, facing us, its doors open like elephant's ears, hiding what was going on behind. I was reluctantly impressed by Jess. While I lurked among the bins she stood out in the middle of the alley, clipboard held out, pen poised, looking round just like someone doing a school project.

A man came out from behind the van's left ear carrying a large brown cardboard box. He went into the door of the empty shop next to the newsagent's. 'Gotcha!' Jess said quietly, and then, 'Why didn't we bring a camera?'

The man came back out of the shop as she spoke and glanced down the alley towards us. He turned and came up, smiling. 'Hello,' he said, 'can I help you?'

Jess switched into charm mode and started gushing about school projects and urban change, patterns of settlement, and retail networks. She must pay attention in school, I thought, impressed. The man seemed impressed too.

'It's these shops,' Jess gushed on. 'Four shops were originally a viable unit, brought trade to each other. The interesting question is, can one survive for long on its own? When did the other shops close?'

The man laughed. 'Search me, love, I'm just delivering,' he said.

I saw Jess suddenly tense. I'd heard her before on what she called 'patronizing put-downs' like 'love' and 'dear', and thought she was about to attack him. Panic opened my mouth, for once.

'Is that one about to reopen?' I said from among the bins. 'The one you're delivering to.'

'Look, this is private property,' he said. 'You can't trespass here. Health and Safety. If there was an accident there'd be real problems. Just leave, will you.' He stood and glared at us and I turned and started walking out. I had got as far as the corner when I heard Jess's voice behind me, too far behind me. She wasn't leaving, quietly and sensibly, as I was. She was standing and arguing. I edged down the alley to the shelter of the bins and tried to attract her attention without being seen.

A second man came out, the man from the shop. 'What's the fuss?' he said, and then obviously recognized Jess. 'You again! What exactly are you playing at?'

'Doing a school project,' Jess said, less confident suddenly. 'Just doing a school project. It's so boring we wanted a fag break earlier.' She sounded almost convincing and should have stopped there. If she had stopped there we could have left peacefully, safely.

As I had got to know Jess over these months I had learnt that she never knew when to stop, she always went too far, in what she did and in what she said. She was always in danger of winding herself up and letting the words spill out without thinking what she was saying. It happened now, and I cringed.

'What could we be playing at? Do you think we're planning to rob your pathetic shop? Do you think we're spying on you? You must spend all your time reading Enid Blyton if you think we're investigating your criminal deeds. What criminal deeds are you up to in this poxy place anyway? Don't tell me you're the mastermind behind illegal immigrant smuggling!'

I saw Jess take a step backwards. I saw the man from

the shop rush up. I saw him grab her. I saw him pick her off the ground and carry her, struggling hopelessly, into the empty shop. The other man followed him and the door banged. I stood, frozen with terror, among the bins.

16

Common Sense and With Hindsight are two amazingly sensible people. If you listen to them you will never get into trouble. Accidents will pass With Hindsight by as he will leave the house two minutes earlier so that the drunk driver will crash into the wall and not into him. Common Sense will not be more than three days late with her homework.

Common Sense and With Hindsight would have kept well out of all the trouble I had landed in. With Hindsight would have been sitting up in the car while his father went to buy fish and chips so that no strange girl would drive their car off. Common Sense would have laughed at the threats the strange girl uttered. Even if they had started down the wrong road, both of them would have told their parents the truth immediately instead of weaving tangles of lies. I was a kamikaze spider, spinning a web to catch itself.

With Hindsight, that smug know-all, was careful never, ever, to be there when things happened. He'd saunter along later, smile condescendingly, and explain slowly, carefully, just what you should have done. Common Sense was less reliable. Sometimes she was around but I reckon she fancied With Hindsight more than she fancied me.

They both now popped their heads out of the wheelie bins and had a good go at me. I knew they were right, but they weren't being exactly helpful, and they kept interrupting each other.

'The sensible thing to do now is . . . ' Common Sense would begin.

'You should never have . . . ' With Hindsight would interrupt.

The trouble with reading books and watching films is that I knew exactly what would happen. I run to the nearest house and bang on the door. A suspicious pensioner opens it, and then slams it in my face. I run to the phone box, and find it vandalized. Eventually I find someone who will listen and pour out my incredible story and persuade them to believe me. They call the police, who eventually believe me too. Van-loads of police descend on the shops. There is no one there except a deaf old lady behind the counter: no van, no men, no boxes, no Jess. Talk your way out of that, Common Sense.

In simple words, I dithered among the dustbins.

The alleyway was quiet. The van sat there with its ears stuck out, listening hard. The litter lay on the ground, unstirred by any wind. I edged out from behind the bins and slid along the wall. I came to the window of the first shop. Grimy glass made it difficult to see in, especially as I was peering from one corner, but it seemed to be empty. I ducked below it just in case and crept on. The next window was the barred one, the one of the empty shop they had carried Jess into.

I tried to look in without being seen. Behind the black lines of the bars the glass reflected back the opposite side of the alley. I squinted at it desperately. Behind the glass there was some kind of curtain. I could see nothing.

If I could see nothing, no one could see me. I ducked down and moved towards the door: solid, with peeling green paint. I looked through the keyhole. I could make out nothing. I listened. There seemed to be people talking but I couldn't hear a single word. I straightened up and looked around.

At the far end of the alleyway there was a pile of rubbish, mainly empty cardboard boxes. I edged under the windows of the last two shops and ran across to it. I pushed my way between the boxes and the wall. The whole heap wobbled and one box fell off the top and bounced on the ground. I froze, expecting the shop door to crash open and the men to rush out. Nothing happened. I let my breath out and moved my head slowly. As long as no one came right up to the wall I should be hidden. The trouble was, so was the alleyway. I could see nothing.

It's easy, I said to myself. It's just like playing with toy bricks. All I have to do is ease a box this way, another that way, and I'll have a peep-hole I can observe through without anyone being able to spot me. But I could see the whole pile collapsing, spilling down the alleyway like an over-ambitious tower of bricks, leaving me standing against the wall, exposed, with nowhere to run.

Look first, act after, I said to myself. I was near the edge of the heap. It looked as if I just had to move one box. I inched my hands out and put one on each side of it. I moved it gently, gently, watching for any movement around it.

There was now a gap. I could see down the alleyway along the side of the van but I couldn't see the shop door. I moved the box a little further. The one next to it started to lean forward, about to fall and start an avalanche. I jerked my right hand instinctively, trying to grab it, and lost control of the box I was holding. Both boxes slid, tottered, settled.

I had a triangular hole through which I could see everything: the alleyway, the shop door, the boxes stacked inside the van. If I kept still I surely wouldn't be noticed. I tried to convince myself that I had done something positive but voices inside my head kept arguing.

All you've done is move from hiding among the dustbins to hiding in a rubbish heap. You've done nothing to help Jess.

83

Jess got herself into this. She can get herself out of it.

You could have walked away months ago, if you'd really wanted to. You didn't. Why not? Could it be you really rather fancy Jess? Could you really have been enjoying a bit of excitement in your rather dull life?

Nothing will happen to Jess.

Anything could happen.

I knew I had to do something. I should have gone for help. I should have been given a mobile when I asked for one. But now? What was I to do now?

The shop door opened. The van driver came out and started moving cardboard boxes out of the van into the shop. I stood and fidgeted. Should I run down the alleyway when he went into the shop? Should I try to get into the shop and free Jess? I did nothing.

When the van was about half empty both men came out and came towards me. They can't know I'm here; they just can't, I told myself, but it was difficult to believe it. They stopped a few feet away from the pile and stood and stared at it, at me.

'They're all the same size,' the driver said. 'She won't fit in. We need one of those boxes fridges come in.'

'Then we'll take two and tape them together,' the shop man said. 'At least they'll match the ones in the van.'

They took a box each from the front of the pile and went back into the shop. I knew now what I had to do, and I knew that I had to do it now. I crept out from behind the boxes and ran towards the van. A neat wall of boxes faced me, but there was a narrow space down the middle. Was it too narrow? I couldn't stop to think. I climbed into the van and pushed my way into the gap. The boxes gave slightly as I squeezed.

At the front of the van there was a gap where the wall met the floor, a sort of upside-down ledge over a toolbox and rags. Somehow I got myself half into this space, and stuck. My feet would be the first thing the men would see as they came to the van.

I panicked, struggled, and the pile of boxes shifted. I pushed and they slid on the floor. I crawled into the space I had made and lay panting. One pile now stuck out in front of the other. I edged back, bent my knees and pushed until the two piles seemed to be level.

Voices came towards the van. Something was dropped on the floor. The doors closed. It was suddenly black. The front door of the van opened and closed. The engine started and we started to move. A thumping noise came from the other side of the boxes.

17

The van slowed, turned, accelerated, slowed, stopped, turned. I tried to keep track of where we were going but I didn't know this part of Oxford and I soon got confused. Anyway, knowing where we were wasn't much help. I needed to talk to Jess.

I squirmed my way back down the narrow gap between the piles. My foot struck the box the men had put in after me. Jess swore. Somehow I didn't like to say anything. I was stupidly afraid that if I spoke the men would hear me above the noise of the engine, the road, the creaking of the boxes. I put my hand out to feel what was there. Cardboard, smooth tape, cardboard: two boxes taped together, as the man had said. I felt down the tape, searching for an end I could pull.

The swearing inside the box was turning to crying. The cool, controlled Jess was cracking up. I couldn't cope with that. I needed her to be in charge, to get us out of this mess. I had to speak. 'It's OK, Jess, I'm here,' I said, my mouth to the tape.

'Where the hell have you been? Get me out of here, you idiot.'

I felt as if I'd been slapped. I'd done brilliantly, heroically, loyally, despite her continual trickery and deceit and sneering. I should have left her to get out of her own mess. I lay there in the dark and sulked.

'Dan, please.'

I couldn't do it. I got my fingernails under the edge of the tape and tugged at it. It was too tough to tear. I couldn't find an end. All I could do was ease it away from one of the boxes. I managed the side nearest me and pushed at the cardboard so that I could reach into the box. My fingers touched Jess.

'Can you pull at the box from the inside?' I said.

'I'd have done it hours ago if I could. They've tied me up. Just get on with it. Get me out!'

I stood up and pulled the tape off the top of the box and edged round the end to do the other side. I still couldn't get Jess out because the tape on the bottom was holding it firmly together. I pushed the cardboard open again. 'I've got to try to turn the boxes over to get at the bottom. Can you roll away from me? Lean on that side?'

'Just get on with it,' Jess said.

Problem number one: there wasn't room to turn the boxes over. Problem number two: I couldn't see what I was doing. Problem number three: the van kept slowing and speeding up and turning so that I was constantly thrown off balance and every time it stopped I was terrified the men would come round, open the doors, and find me. I pushed the top of the boxes as far as it would go and wedged my feet underneath to stop them dropping back. Then I crouched down and pulled the bottom towards me. Jess's weight kept them standing on one edge. I steadied them with one hand and pulled at the tape with the other.

They were separated, but there wasn't enough room to pull them apart. The van slowed down and I panicked. 'It's no good! They won't come apart!' I cried and yanked at them. They thumped back on to the floor of the van. Jess yelled:

'Stop! Calm down!'

I stopped pulling. The van sped up again. We seemed to think together. I pushed the boxes as far back as they would go and then went to the side of the van and pushed the boxes over one way. Jess's voice came out of the blackness.

'If I squeeze into this box, then try moving the other.'

The left-hand box shook as she moved into it. I lifted the right-hand one upwards and forwards as easy as easy.

'Get me untied,' Jess said. I knelt down and reached out my fingers. They touched her hair, her face. I moved my hands down, feeling for what was holding her.

'I knew you fancied me,' she said, 'but this is taking unfair advantage.' Her mocking coolness was back and I was glad. It was easier to cope with than her desperation.

There was more parcel tape round her wrists and round her ankles. I couldn't feel an end to pull. I couldn't tear it. I had no handy Swiss army knife. Then I remembered the toolbox. It was even more difficult to move in the van now, with Jess and her two boxes added to the darkness and the lurching of the van. I wormed along until I could stretch out my arm and feel for the toolbox and pull it back after me. I sat up and opened it and put my hand in, very cautiously. I was afraid of grabbing a saw or a chisel.

My fingers felt a smooth round tube. I picked it up, found a switch, and we had light at last. Jess's face was a startled paleness. Her hair merged into the darkness around.

'Stop shining that in my eyes and get me untied, idiot,' she said, but 'idiot' was friendlier now. I shone the torch into the toolbox and found a craft knife and cut through the tape round her wrists. She stretched out her arms, pulled my head towards her, and kissed me. 'Now my feet,' she said.

She sat up and was in charge again. 'Shine the torch in the toolbox.' She picked up the largest spanner and waved it threateningly at me. 'Right, we're ready for them. Let's see if we can get out of this thing.'

She took the torch from me and pointed the beam at the door. There was no nice shiny chrome door handle sticking out saying 'Open me!' 'There must be one,' Jess said.

'Suppose you were in here and the wind blew the door shut.' She moved towards the back and then said, 'Got it!'

There was a click and one of the doors swung open and daylight dazzled in. Jess grabbed at the door. I grabbed at her, terrified she would roll out and I would see her bounce along the road behind. We lay on the floor of the van looking out at hedges and fields unwinding behind us. 'Where are we?'

'More to the point, what are we going to do?' Jess said. 'That's another question we don't have an answer to. And just to make things worse, I've got to shut this door; my arms can't take any more.' We were back in darkness and I felt my heart sink. Sooner or later the van would stop. The men would come round and open the doors. We would be discovered. I didn't really believe that a craft knife and a spanner would be much use against them. I couldn't see myself actually slashing at someone's face, but what else could we do?

Jess snapped at me when I said this. She said I was a complete idiot. Didn't I realize that we had surprise on our side? The men thought I was miles away, if they thought about me at all, which wasn't likely as I was, apparently, such a useless little wimp. They thought Jess was tied up inside the boxes.

'Plan A,' she said, 'we jump out as soon as they open the doors and make a run for it. We'll be well away before they know what's happened.'

'Suppose they drive the van into a garage and shut its doors first? We'd have nowhere to run to.' My trouble is I watch too much TV.

'When the van slows down we open the door a crack and see where we are. If they slow down enough we can jump out anyway.' I could just see that: leap out of a moving vehicle, fall over, break a leg.

'Plan B?'

'Plan B: we stick the boxes together again as best we can, put another box in to make it feel as if I'm still inside, and then hide behind the piles. They'll carry what they think is me away and we can slip off quietly while they're not looking.'

I suddenly remembered something. 'Where's your mobile?'

'They took it off me, of course. Where's yours?' That was mean of her because she knew I wasn't allowed one. 'Well, what are we going to do?'

I couldn't face squirming back into that little space, knowing there was no way out, just hoping the men would be stupid enough not to realize Jess wasn't in the boxes. There was no real choice.

'Plan A,' I said.

18

Waiting was hard. I felt my courage oozing away as I sat there. Jess must have felt the same because she suddenly said, 'Shine the torch in the toolbox!' I felt round for where I had left it and switched it on. Jess said, 'I thought so!' and picked up a roll of parcel tape. 'We'll prepare Plan B just in case.'

She was right. It gave us the feeling that we were doing something, fighting back. We picked up one of the full boxes and wedged it into the empty one. 'It's too light,' Jess said. 'Even my perfect figure weighs more than that.' She picked up the toolbox and taped it to the floor of the other empty box. We then manoeuvred them together and put new tape over the old where I had eased it off. It was easier with two of us, and the torch. Then we straightened the boxes up and sat and waited.

We didn't have to wait long. The van slowed, turned, and stopped before we realized that it wasn't just driving through traffic. We heard one of the front doors open and felt the bang of the passenger door shutting. I gripped the craft knife until my hand hurt and stood tensed, ready to jump out and run. Where to? We had no plan for this. Did we run together, or split up? We heard scraping noises behind, and then the van started reversing, throwing me off balance and against the boxes. It stopped again before I was ready.

The driver's door opened and shut. Voices spoke words I couldn't turn into sense. There were those scraping sounds again. There was silence.

I felt stupid standing there, knife in hand. Suppose the men had just abandoned the van. It could have been stolen. They might just leave it, and Jess. But would they leave the boxes? Perhaps they were empty. Perhaps other men were coming for it. Perhaps they were waiting for dark. We could be waiting, poised, for hours. Jess must have been thinking the same because she said, 'We've got to open the door.'

'Where are we going to run to?' I asked, stupidly. How did we know where we were going when we didn't even know where we were?

'We'll keep together unless I shout "Split!"' she said. 'If you escape and I don't then you must phone the police straightaway. Must! Ready?'

She pushed the spanner at me. I nearly said I didn't need it but then realized that she wanted both hands free. I heard the click of the catch on the door and tensed even more. There was a pause and then she edged the door open a crack. Light came in, not as dazzling as before but enough to see Jess leaning forward, peering.

She eased the door a fraction more. 'There's a wall behind us. We're in some kind of shed or garage. I can't hear anything. Let's go, slowly and very quietly.'

She pushed the door so that it was wide enough to get out. She stretched out her hand for the spanner and stepped out of the van. I could now see cobwebby bricks and oil stains on a concrete floor. Above us was a rusty corrugated iron roof. I got out. Jess was looking round the end of the van. 'Shut the door,' she said, without turning round and moved out of sight. I closed the door as quietly as I could and quickly followed her. Ahead of us were wooden doors with dirty windows at the top. The doors were shut.

'Help steady me,' Jess said. She climbed on to the bumper of the van and then on to the bonnet. She leant forward and looked out of the window, cautiously at first and then openly. 'No one in sight,' she said. 'There's a yard, with a wall to the left, then a gate on to the road.' She jumped down. 'Let's do it before they come back. We open the door, go left along the wall, out of the gate, and turn left. If they come after us you go left and I'll go right. Get to a phone. Dial 999.'

She pushed at the right-hand door. It moved, scraping on the ground. She stopped and swore. 'We might as well shout, "We're escaping!"'

'Lift it,' I said.

'Right, Samson, you lift it,' she snapped. Her calm organized surface had slipped again.

There wasn't anything to hold to lift the door with. I crouched down and tried to get my fingers underneath but the door was resting on the ground. I put my fingers through the tiny gap that had opened up and held on to the front edge of the door. 'I'll try and lift while you push. Do it slowly.'

This time the scraping was quieter. We got the door just wide enough to squeeze through and came out into the yard. There was no one about and safety was just across a small yard. 'Leave the door,' Jess said, back into I'm-the-boss mode. 'With luck they'll just think that's how they left it. Let's go.'

It was difficult. I wanted just to sprint straight across to the gate, to get away, but common sense insisted that it was safer to walk slowly round the edge, and for once I listened to common sense. We crept along the wall. I kept wanting to look back but forced myself to look ahead. We reached the corner and turned towards the gate. Out of the corner of my eye I could see what looked like a small derelict factory building next to the garage.

We reached the gate, went through, and stepped on to the pavement. It felt like feeling sand under your feet after hours fighting cold waves. 'Cross the road,' Jess said. We walked over, dodging the traffic, like normal people. There was a bus stop just down the road with two women waiting. 'Brilliant!' Jess said. 'There must be a bus due.'

'Where to? Where are we?'

'It doesn't matter. We'll just vanish, and sort ourselves out later.'

We walked down to the stop. I couldn't help glancing back every few paces. No one was after us, yet. The women knew what they were doing: a bus pulled in to the stop as we reached it. It had 'Oxford' in its indicator window. Jess bought us tickets—'At least they didn't steal my money,' she said—and we sat and looked out of the window as the bus drove past the yard with its garage. Nothing had changed.

'I'd still be in there, in that box, if it wasn't for you,' Jess said. 'I owe you one. Now we've got to get my phone back.'

I stared at her. Was she completely mad? Was this what she called owing me one? 'We?' I said.

'Look, it couldn't be safer. We know where the men are. That shop is the last place they'll expect to find me. Please, Dan. I'll be in such trouble if Dad finds out I've lost another phone. I'm in trouble enough at home as it is. All I need is a lookout.'

'I need to get home,' I said. 'I'll be in trouble too. Mum'll be expecting me.'

'No, she won't. I had a nice chat to her on the phone this morning. She thinks you're with me all day. She approves of me; she's the only person who does. Come on, please. You're so brilliant. This'll be the last time, I promise. If I have to go home without the phone everything will come out, I know it will. Everything.'

So much for owing me one, I thought again, bitterly. She'd never stop blackmailing me into doing whatever crazy thing she wanted. At least I didn't feel I owed her anything. I'd call her bluff. My mistake had been to be too brilliant; that's why she wouldn't let me go. I was perfect for her: weak-willed but efficient. I'd have to make her see that I was unreliable and then she'd give up on me. I'd pretend to go along with it, wait till she was in the shop, and then just walk off. She surely couldn't get me into trouble with her photos; she'd be in too much herself.

'OK,' I said. 'If you insist. But I'm not coming in. I'll keep watch, and that's all.'

'Great,' she said, and leant across and kissed me. It was getting to be a habit with her, and one I could do without, particularly when the two women behind started talking about us in a very embarrassing way. One last time, I said to myself.

19

It didn't quite go as Jess had planned. By the time the bus had crawled back into Oxford through all the traffic I was so hungry that I refused to do anything until I'd had something to eat. The morning's lemon cake was a long time ago. Jess said that the quickest thing was to go to her house, make a sandwich which we could eat on a bus going back to the row of shops and our bikes. I had forgotten my bike was there. I had to fetch it, so really I had no choice about going back.

'We could buy a sandwich here,' I said.

'How much money have you got?'

We set off for Jess's house. I had enough money for half a sandwich and Jess had either suddenly gone mean after paying the bus fares, or really didn't have much money left. I couldn't complain after all the coffees and cakes she'd bought me. Anyway, I was desperate for food, and I really didn't want to go back to the shop at all.

We were within sight of Jess's house when the man came out of nowhere and grabbed us both. I was too startled to do anything but Jess wriggled free and turned and faced him. He tightened his grip on my arm. Now I noticed, too late, his white van parked down the road.

'What do you want?' Jess said.

'I don't want to hurt you,' Steve Grafton said. 'I just need a word with you and your boyfriend. You wrote me a letter a while ago. I know it was you, so don't try denying it. It's those kids, I thought, forget it. Then when I saw you just now I thought, I won't have them sticking their noses into my business. So, this is just a friendly word of advice about mouths, about keeping them shut. You wouldn't want it hurt, would you, not your boyfriend's mouth, or your girlfriend's? Wouldn't do a lot for the snogging, would it?'

'Are you interested in a van-load of cigarettes?' Jess said.

'What do you mean?'

'We can take you to where some smugglers have stored all their cigarettes. You can take them, and then we'll be accessories, criminals with you. You'd know then that we could never tell the police because we'd be in trouble too.'

Typical Jess, I thought. She thinks that the way to control people is to involve them in something wrong. He stood looking at her. 'You think this is some kind of joke,' he said. 'Well, I'm not joking. You two have got to be shut up, starting now.'

'I'm not joking,' Jess said. 'We know where there's a building full of smuggled cigarettes. That's a certainty. Probably, the men aren't there. We can take you there. You can fill your van up. They've broken the law, so they're not likely to go to the police. They'll have no idea who you are. The perfect crime.'

'Tell me more,' he said at last. 'What are you doing mixed up in it?'

'It's a long story,' she said. 'But these men have stolen my mobile phone,' she said. 'We were going to break in to their hiding place and get it back. And our bikes are there. If we come with you, in your van, we can show you where all the cigarettes are. I'll get my phone. You'll get a load of cigarettes, no questions asked. And if you pay us something for the information then we certainly couldn't tell the police, could we. I'll give you a receipt if you like: "I, Jane Morgan, have received £100 for freely giving Mr Stephen Grafton information to his advantage,"—something like that.'

Typical Jess, I thought. 'A hundred's ridiculous,' the man said, hooked.

'What's a van load of free cigarettes worth to you? Thousands! And the more you pay us, the more guilty we are, the more we're obviously in it for the money and not because you threatened us.' She smiled at him.

'We'll go and have a look,' he said. 'I'm not promising anything. And don't try anything silly. I don't want anyone to get hurt.'

'What about some food?' I said. Jess looked at me as if I was a complete idiot.

'I've got some biscuits in the van,' he said. Great, I thought, what happened to all those warnings about strange men in cars offering sweets?

'OK,' Jess said. 'Biscuits to fill his mouth, £100 cash to shut mine, and my phone back. Sounds good to me.' It sounded absolutely stupid to me but no one was interested in what I thought. We went over to the van. 'I'll come in the front with you,' Jess said, 'so that I can show you where to go.'

He opened the back door and I climbed in. I didn't seem to have any choice. It was much smaller than the other van and there was no partition separating the back from the two seats in front, which made me feel safer. He passed a packet of biscuits over to me and we set off. Jess told him where to go and was then silent until we'd crossed Magdalen Bridge.

'Have you got the cash?' she asked.

'I get the cigarettes; you get the cash. That's the deal. I hope for all our sakes you do.' Silence fell again. I was uncomfortable in the back. There was a pile of old dust sheets like painters use to sit on but I had to brace myself to stop falling off. If I leant against the side I was jolted unpleasantly.

At last we turned off into Blakeney Road and he drove

slowly down while Jess pointed out the row of shops and the alleyway next to them. He turned left into the main road, went left and left again and pulled into the kerb at the top of Blakeney Road.

'You're sure there's no one there?'

'Try the shop,' Jess said. 'If that's shut, have a look in the alleyway. If there's no van, then there's no one.'

'Alarms?'

'Would you have an alarm where you store your loot? Look, there's a box on the shop but I bet that's just for show. And even if the shop itself is alarmed, you're going in next door. Just walk along and have a look.'

'While you two get on your bikes and disappear?'

'Without my hundred pounds?' The trouble was, I knew she meant it, and I think the man did too. 'Look, here is my bike padlock key. Henry, give him yours.' I reluctantly handed mine over as ordered. Jess wasn't going to let me go, whatever my name was, so I might as well.

He got out of the van and walked down to the shop, stopped and peered in, and then went past and disappeared into the alleyway.

'What's this "Henry"?' I asked.

'Sometimes, Daniel, you are so stupid I don't know why I bother with you. You're Henry and I'm Jane and don't forget it. Just be thankful I can think for both of us. Revenge, and a hundred pounds, and the man off our backs; that can't be bad. And be thankful that I didn't call you "Tarzan".' She was obviously feeling very pleased with herself.

Steve Grafton came back and got into the van. 'There doesn't seem to be anyone there,' he said. 'Where are these cigarettes, then?' Jess explained about the empty shop second along. He sat and thought and then said, 'Right, I need you two as lookouts. I'll go and park the van near the entrance to the alleyway and go and open up. You'll stay in the van. If you see your friends coming blast the horn and get out of sight under the sheets in the back. I'll come out looking innocent and drive off.'

'If they don't come?'

'Once I've opened up and checked what's there, I'll back the van round. Henry here can wait on the pavement across the road opposite and you stand in the corner of the alley. If they come, then Henry waves to you and walks down the road, you run and tell me and jump into the van. I drive off and hope to get out before they arrive. If not, I'm just an innocent van driver looking for Henry's Hardware to make a delivery. And then we pick up Henry here as we go past. OK?'

'Get my phone out, Steve,' Jess said. 'When you go in first. It's on a table at the back of the room. Otherwise if it gets left there they can find out who I am and we'll have them after me instead of you.'

'I don't know how you put up with her, Henry,' he said. 'She'd be too bossy for me.' And me, I thought, but I didn't say it out loud.

'Let's get on with it then,' he said, and started the engine.

20

Steve Grafton stopped just past the corner. 'Right, Jane, you use the mirror to look behind. Can you see down the road?' Jess nodded. I still couldn't think why she had given him false names, except that she was just a liar by nature. It did, somehow, make the whole nightmare less real. 'Good. That's the most likely way they'll come. Henry, you look straight ahead. Any sign, hoot. Don't wait to be sure. If you think it might be them, hoot, get under the sheets, and don't move.'

He leant forward and reached under his seat. When he sat up again he was holding a small cloth bag. 'See you in a couple of minutes.'

'Don't forget my phone, Steve,' Jess said. 'And there's a clipboard by it. I'd like that back as well. I only bought it this morning.'

'Please!' he said, and shut the van door.

'We ought to go,' I said.

'No phone, no clipboard, no bikes, no hundred pounds? You're such an idiot sometimes. Why did I ever think I could train you up into something useful? There's no way we're going now. Just keep a good lookout.'

The road was quiet, eerily so. It was like one of those westerns where everyone goes indoors before the gunfight down the main street. The rain, which had been threatening all day, started falling, pinging on the roof of the van and making it difficult to see out of the windscreen. It wasn't going to be much fun standing by the side of the road. I almost hoped the van would come now. It would be worse for Jess, though. She could be caught in the alleyway with nowhere to run.

'There's a pile of boxes at the end of the alleyway,' I said. 'You can squeeze behind and hide if they come. You don't have to get in his van again.' Jess didn't answer. She never liked me knowing more than she did, or having any useful ideas. We sat in silence. I stared ahead at the empty road.

He came back and got in the van. He passed Jess her clipboard. 'Thanks,' she said. 'Where's my phone?'

He patted his pocket. 'Safe in here. You get it back later. Call it a hostage.'

'Like the hundred pounds,' Jess said. He laughed. He seemed to find Jess funny, but then he didn't know her, hadn't suffered from her bright ideas.

'It's all open,' he said. 'We'd better get on with it. Henry on the road; Jane at the corner. Sorry about the rain. I'll be as quick as I can, don't worry.'

'Give us our bike keys, please,' said Jess. 'If we have to make a run for it we'll be much safer. You've got my phone, and my money, as hostage.'

'Fair enough. You'll be in sight every time I come out to the van, so don't think of making a run for it or I'll be after you.' He took our keys out of his pocket and passed them to her. She put them both in her pocket.

'I'll give you yours when you need it, Henry,' she said. 'I don't want you thinking about slipping off and leaving me in the alleyway.'

'Honour among thieves,' he laughed again, and came round to open the back of the van. 'Out you get, Henry, and don't forget: you're the one we're all relying on and I know where you live, as they say.' Except you don't, I thought, and felt a small satisfaction.

I walked across the road and stood sheltering pathetically behind a lamp-post. The van started up and reversed down the alleyway and out of sight round the corner. I looked in panic up and down the road. Jess was still in the van. If the other men came now I wouldn't be able to signal. I'd have to run across the road, shouting. They'd accelerate, run me over . . .

Jess appeared at the corner of the alleyway and waved at me. I waved back, and then thought that perhaps I shouldn't have. We hadn't arranged any signals. If the van came, when the van came, was I going to wave? Would she just think I was being friendly? How was I going to warn her without also alerting the men driving down the road?

The rain eased, and then stopped. I stood dripping and worrying. I could hear the traffic on the main roads at each end but Blakeney Road itself was quiet, deserted. Then against the background traffic I heard a vehicle turning towards me and stiffened. It was a green car. As it got closer I could see a woman driving it. She looked at me, as if wondering what I was doing lurking about and I panicked again. Was there a Neighbourhood Watch? Had some alert pensioner already rung the police to report a suspicious youth hanging about? When the police car drove up, did I signal to Jess to get out, or to hide? And how would I explain that I was the innocent lookout for a man stealing smuggled cigarettes? Why hadn't Jess and I worked out a code of signals? I wanted her to wave reassuringly at me, to tell me it was almost over, but I daren't move in case she misunderstood me.

It must be almost over. How long could it take to put those big cartons into a small van? At least Jess could see what was going on. I was just stuck out in the road, in full view, with nothing to do. I should have had the clipboard. I could have pretended to be sketching the shops. I could go and fetch it, see how things were going, and be back here before anything could happen. But that would be the one moment the van drove up. I would come out of the alleyway straight into their van.

A car came, from the opposite direction. It was the same car coming back. It slowed, and the woman looked at me. I smiled, sort of, and that seemed to frighten her off. She drove very slowly down the road. I could imagine her watching me in her mirror. I tried to look innocent. I had a perfect right to stand by the side of the road for as long as I wanted. I wasn't doing any harm, as far as she knew.

I watched her stop at the end of the road and turn left. There it was! The van, it must be. I waved frantically at Jess and saw her run down the alleyway. I turned and walked along the road with my back to the approaching men. The shop man had seen me when we first went in. He could recognize me. I must not run. I must not look back.

The van passed me. It was the wrong colour. It was the wrong van.

I ran back, back towards them. I had to tell them it was a false alarm before they screeched out, doors open, Jess running behind and trying to jump in. I would have to go into the alleyway, to tell them.

There was a van coming towards me, the smugglers' van. There was our van, Steve Grafton's van, coming round the corner of the alleyway. I stood, frozen. 'Run!' my mind said, but my legs refused. Their van, it really was their van this time, signalled and turned across the road. The vans met, stopped. I managed to shuffle a few steps backwards.

The passenger door opened and the shop man got out. He walked across to Steve's van and leant down to talk to him. I couldn't quite hear what they said but the shop man straightened up and started pointing like someone giving directions. I edged back a few more steps. It was going to be all right.

The shop man bent down again to say something else. I think he must have seen the cartons piled up inside the van and said something. Steve's van suddenly jerked forward, making the shop man leap back. It turned sharp right and drove along the pavement. It swerved round a lamp-post on to the road and accelerated away. The shop man ran back to his van, got in, and it drove away in pursuit. I stood and watched them both drive down the road.

21

He was supposed to stop and pick me up. He and Jess were driving off. I was miles from home, on the wrong side of Oxford. Jess had my bike keys and I didn't have enough money for the bus fare. I'd just had a couple of biscuits for lunch, which wasn't much to walk home on.

I was on my own and had to sort myself out. What about Jess? Should I ring the police? If I did, what would I tell them? I stood on the pavement, looking down the now empty road, trying to think what I could say that would sound convincing. I couldn't even remember the number of either van. The numbers were written on Jess's clipboard. 'A white van and a blue van' wasn't much for them to go on. I tried to persuade myself that this time she wasn't in any real danger. Our man, White Van Man, seemed in fact pretty reasonable, seemed to like Jess, would look after her. It was Blue Van Men who were dangerous, and they hadn't got her. Not yet, Worry said. In the middle of Oxford? I asked it. In the middle of the afternoon?

'Dan!'

I turned. There was Jess, coming out of the alleyway, clutching her clipboard. I felt a stupid grin coming on my face as I ran over the road towards her. 'I thought you were in the van.'

'I took your advice and hid behind the boxes when you waved. He drove off in such a hurry I don't think he knew whether I was in the van or not. What happened?'

I described the way the two vans had met, and how they

had driven down the road and out of sight. 'So much for my hundred quid,' she said. 'And my mobile.' I managed to stop myself saying, I told you so. I thought now wasn't quite the moment, not while she still had my bike keys. 'We'd better go home,' she said, which was about the first sensible thing she'd said since I'd first known her. Perhaps there was some hope she might one day turn into a normal person.

We walked down the road towards our bikes. A white van turned into the road and pulled up next to us. Jess went round to the driver's window. 'Thanks for coming back,' she said. 'I'd like my mobile, *please*, and my money.'

'Nearly there,' he said. 'I can fit two more cartons in. We'll just get them quickly then we can be off and settle up.' We? Did he really think that we'd go back with the thugs now alert to what was going on? 'I'll park by the entrance and keep the engine running. You two nip in and bring out a box each. If I see them coming I'll drive off. They'll follow me, I'll lose them again and come round and pick you up. Don't worry, with all the traffic lights round here it's not difficult to get rid of someone following you. If I drive off, hide the boxes behind a parked car for safety.'

I waited for Jess to explode but she meekly said, 'OK. Come on, Dan.'

'Dan?' he said. 'I thought his false name was Henry, Jane?' and he laughed. He drove the van over the road to just past the entrance to the alleyway. Jess set off after him and I followed her reluctantly. I didn't seem to have much choice.

We walked down to the corner by the bins. 'You go and get two boxes out,' I said. 'I'll keep a lookout.'

'Don't be silly, Dan,' Jess said. It seemed to be her favourite expression at the moment. I followed her along and into the back of the empty shop. This must have been a storeroom behind the actual shop and it still had wide wooden shelves from floor to ceiling. Now it certainly wasn't empty. Cardboard cartons practically filled the small space, though there was a van-sized space by the door. Jess picked up a carton and carried it out. 'Time to put your burglary skills to use again, Dan,' she said.

I picked up a carton and followed her out and down the alley. We got to the corner in time to see our van drive off with a squeal of tyres. 'Hide!' Jess yelled and threw her carton behind the wheelie bins and ran after it. I pushed in next to her. This was a stupid place to hide. If they came into the alleyway they'd see us and we'd be blocked in. It would be better to hide at the end, behind the empty boxes. But I couldn't move. Jess was peering between a bin and the wall.

'Here they come,' she said. I could hear the sound of a diesel engine clunking on the road, but getting no closer. 'They're not falling for it,' Jess said. 'They're not following him.'

I tugged at her. 'Let's go and hide.'

If we stayed where we were we'd be seen. There was no chance, no real chance, they could just drive past the bins and not spot us, even if we crouched down or flattened ourselves against the wall. If we moved there was a chance they'd see us, but the wheelie bin might hide us while we slipped round the corner.

'We've got to go!' I said. And Jess had to come with me. Somehow I needed her to make the first move, to break the spell. Finally she turned and edged past me, and round the corner. I followed, expecting yells and the revving of the engine but it stayed throbbing away on the road.

Jess paused at the entrance to their store and looked in. 'Here,' she said. I stood and stared at her. Was she mad? 'It's the last place they'll look. Behind the empty boxes is a death-trap. It's too obvious. If they look. But I don't think they know we're here at all.'

The engine noise changed, grew louder, closer. 'Come on!' she said, and went inside. I followed. I had to. Jess went over to the wall of boxes and scrambled up it. They had been stacked carelessly so that there were footholds in places like very narrow stairs. Jess went up as if she'd been doing it all her life, lay on the top and stretched her hand down. I grasped it and somehow managed to clamber up beside her.

The van was closer now. Its bulk blocked out the light that was coming through the open door, plunging us into deep shadow. We slithered over the top of the boxes. The roof was just above us with a strip light sticking down that we had to go round. I got to the back of the room and I saw what Jess had seen before. The boxes weren't pushed up against the back wall. They were pushed against the wide wooden shelves, and the top shelf was below the top of the boxes. Jess rolled on to it. I had a nightmare vision of the shelf collapsing, on to the one below, and the one below that, down to the ground, with the noise bringing the men rushing in.

There was a slight creak. I slid over and eased myself down so we were lying head to head. There were two slams and I tensed myself, thinking the shelf was going under my weight but it wasn't moving. When I heard the voices I realized that the men had got out of the van and were coming in. We were out of sight and safe unless they moved all the boxes—or one of us sneezed in the dust that had swirled up from the shelf when we had landed on it.

Jess was lifting her head to peer over. I put out my hand and pushed her down. The men would be looking round to see what our man had been doing and would see her.

The strip light buzzed and came on. The men obviously didn't like what they saw. They swore and then the shop man said, 'No good crying over spilt milk. All the more reason to get this lot shifted. That kid could be on to the police.'

The noises were unmistakable now. The men were picking up boxes and carrying them out to the van. I looked at Jess. 'They won't fit in the van in one go,' she whispered.

'You've counted, have you?'

The noises continued. I lay and panicked. I hoped Jess was dreaming up some wonder plan because I certainly couldn't. I was waiting for the moment when one of the men moved the box in front of me and looked straight into my eyes.

22

'We've got the advantage,' Jess whispered. Some advantage, I thought, as I heard the boxes being moved closer and closer to where I was. I could now be safely hidden behind the empties. I could now be happily at home. 'They don't know we're here. We're going to run for it when I say "Go!" They'll be so surprised that they won't be able to catch us. Duck and dodge and you'll get through. At the road, you go left, I'll go right. Whoever gets away rings the police. Straightaway. No amateur heroics like last time.' That's typical, I thought. I save her from the mess she gets herself into and I'm in the wrong. I save her from the mess she gets herself into and she immediately gets herself back into the same mess.

Jess went on whispering. It wasn't anything useful and just wound me up. I hate people whispering and now I worried that the men would hear and would be ready for us. They might know we were here anyway. They might have seen us behind the wheelie bin. They might have checked behind the empties and seen we weren't there. They would know that there was only one place we could be. They would be ready for us to make a move. The van might be wedged across the alleyway so that there was no way past. We'd run out and find there was nowhere to go.

The last but one box was moved from in front of me. Jess shut up at last. I suddenly saw another problem. They were taking one box at a time. One of us might get out but the other would still be stuck, blocked in, waiting to be dragged out. And one box-width wasn't going to give me space to make a run for it, just a space to make an awkward crawl. I needed to hide until at least two boxes had gone. I edged back towards the corner.

Jess turned her head and looked at me. I had moved too far from her for her to be able to whisper. The box immediately in front of where my head and shoulders had been moved away. Jess realized then what I was doing and started sliding back towards her corner. Another box went. Any moment now I would have to go, if I could make myself move. I looked across at Jess. She held up one finger. One more box? One minute?

I could hear the voices of the two men outside in the alleyway. Now was the time. Now, or wait to be found. I crawled forward to the gap and moved on to the box. The men were still outside. I jumped from the box to the floor. Jess landed next to me, pushing me off balance. I grabbed at her to steady myself, nearly pulling her over. We moved cautiously to the barred and dirty window and tried to see out. The blue side of the van filled it completely. We edged along the wall and stood behind the door.

Jess put her mouth to my ear. 'Wait until they come in. Once they're past us, run!' I nodded. I knew that meeting a man in the doorway was the very worst thing that could happen. But what if one came in and the other was outside?

Jess whispered again. 'I think they're in the van. I'm going to have a look.' She took two quick steps across the doorway to the shadow on the other side. I kept one hand on the door but moved so that I could see what she was doing. She stretched her neck, leaning forward so that she looked as if she'd topple forwards. She jerked back and signalled violently at me to join her. I forced myself through the light to her side.

'They're straightening the boxes in the van,' she breathed. 'Let's go. Slowly and silently.'

She moved out. I kept as close to her as I could. The first out will catch their attention, I thought, and they'll catch the second. I could see for myself now in the brightness outside. The van was backed up straight. There was a gap along its side. Noises came from inside of boxes being moved. I wanted to run but Jess was tiptoeing so slowly. I pushed her to get her to hurry.

I must have caught her off-balance again because she lurched to the right. She put her hand out to steady herself and I heard it knock on the side of the van. 'What was that?' one of the men said. Jess at last started running and I ran after her. 'It's those kids,' the shop man shouted, and I heard footsteps coming after us.

We turned the corner, passed the bins and the two cardboard boxes. There in front of us, on the road at the end of the alleyway, was the white van. Steve Grafton swung the passenger door open and yelled, 'Get in! Quick!' Somehow both of us fell into the front and he swung the van violently away from the kerb. There was a thump on the roof and the door banged shut.

I managed to disentangle myself from Jess and slid down on to the floor, squeezing myself in next to her legs. I was panting and shaking and I could feel Jess was trembling too.

'Cut it a bit fine, didn't you?' he said. I suddenly thought how weird it was that I was relieved to be sitting on the floor of a burglar's van. 'Got my two boxes, then?'

'We got them out, just,' Jess said. 'They're hidden behind the bins. You get them if you want them.'

I couldn't see where we were going. We weren't going anywhere much, I thought. The van was moving slowly and he seemed to be turning a lot of corners. I was beginning to feel slightly sick. At last he pulled in and switched the engine off.

'They're not following,' he said. 'What happened?'

Jess told him, roughly. In her version incredible cleverness and bravery was shown by one of us while the other caused all the problems, but I couldn't be bothered to correct her. Steve seemed amused enough.

'So they're going to drive off with their van-load? We'd better watch them go and you can then rescue those two cartons before the bin men decide to make a collection.'

'You can do that,' Jess said. 'We've done enough. Just give me my mobile and the money and we'll be off.'

'The trouble is,' he said, 'those two cartons are your cut. The profit on those is what will pay you. No cartons, no cut.' When Jess started protesting he interrupted her, saying, 'Besides, you're so brilliant at out-witting an international gang of cigarette smugglers that just picking up two boxes and carrying them a couple of yards won't trouble you, will it?'

Jess sat muttering. 'We'll go round,' Steve said. 'I don't think they'll have finished loading yet, according to what you say, so we'll park well back and just have a look. Trust me. I don't want you getting into trouble. It won't do me any good. We'll take it slow and careful.'

He started the engine and drove off. We must have been very close because it wasn't long before he stopped again. 'I need to move,' I said. 'I'm getting cramp.' Jess moved over and I managed to fit myself between her and Steve, half on the seat and half on the handbrake. We were parked near the end of Blakeney Road. Several parked cars blocked the view down the road but I could just make out where the row of shops was, and where the alleyway must be. We'd certainly see their big blue van if it drove out.

We sat in silence for a while. I was almost past being frightened. I wanted to go home but this ordeal seemed to be stretching out for ever. Jess spoke first. She couldn't ever sit still for long. 'So, the van drives out. You pull up to the shops. We get the boxes and put them in the back of the van. You give me my mobile and my money. You drive off and we never see you again. That's the deal, right?'

'Sounds pretty fair to me,' he said.

'And if the boxes aren't there any longer?'

'You get your phone. I drive off and you never see me again.'

'That's not fair,' Jess said. 'You wouldn't have anything if it wasn't for me. I'm out of pocket on this: clipboard, bus fares . . .'

'Fair enough,' he said. 'One hundred if you get the two boxes in the van. Seventy-five for one box. Fifty if they've gone.'

'There's the van,' Jess said.

23

'How many in the van?' Steve asked but neither of us had been able to see. We watched it drive away from us down the road. One of the men had certainly gone, but where was the other? Was he lurking about, ready to pounce? But there could surely only be one man left, at most, and there were three of us. And if I went into the alleyway expecting someone to be there I'd be poised ready to run, and it wouldn't be me he caught.

'Right,' he said, 'no mucking about. If the boxes aren't where you left them, come straight back. Don't try going back into the shop again.'

He drove the van forward and stopped just before the alleyway. He got out and went to the back and opened the door. Then he came round to our side and opened our door. 'Off you go,' he said. 'I'll sit in ready to drive. You walk down, pick up a box each, put them in the back, shut the door, get in, and we'll be away. Safe and simple.'

I followed Jess, ready to make a run for it. There, pushed against the wall by the bins, were the two cartons. We picked them up and hurried back to the van. Steve had been right: they just fitted, with some pushing. Jess shut the door and we got back in the front, me in the middle again.

'We'll move from here and then settle up,' Steve Grafton said. He drove off, turned right, and found a parking place on the main road near our bikes. He took a wallet out of his inside jacket pocket and counted out five twenty-pound notes. 'I want a receipt,' he said.

116

'Ha, ha,' Jess said, stretching her hand across. She was obviously worried Steve might give me the money.

'I'm serious,' he said. 'Pick up your clipboard you were so worried about and write.' He waited while Jess scrabbled on the floor until she'd got the board and her pen. 'Received one hundred pounds—and put that in words not figures—as payment for help in stealing cigarettes from shop in Blakeney Road. Date, sign it, and print your name underneath. Your proper name, the one you've got on the back of your phone, Jess.'

She had to lean forward to be able to move her arm enough to write. When she had finished she tore the sheet of paper off and passed it over. He read it, folded it into quarters, and pushed it down into his side pocket. Then he passed the notes over to her. 'Good to do business with you,' he said. 'You keep quiet now, and keep your boyfriend here quiet, and you won't have any more trouble from me.' He passed her mobile over. 'No sign of trouble out there,' he said. 'I'd get going, if I were you.'

Jess opened the van door and got out. As I put my hand down to edge across the seat I touched a folded piece of paper. Jess's receipt. In the squash he had missed his pocket. I folded my hand round it and got out. As we walked to our bikes I put it into my pocket. At last I had my insurance against Jess. Never again would I have to help with her stupid games because she threatened to expose me. I didn't think he would bother about it. If he'd really wanted it he would have put it in his wallet. It was just a way of frightening us. Either he'd forget all about it or he'd just think he'd dropped it somewhere.

We cycled back in silence. Now that it was over I felt cold and shaky. I couldn't believe that it had really happened, and I couldn't believe that it was all over. We stopped at the end of Jess's road. 'Thanks, Dan,' she said. 'You were great, really. Forget the horrid things I said. I won't see you for a bit because we're going away, but I'll be in touch. Here, this is for you.'

She took the money out of her pocket and gave it to me. 'You have this,' she said. 'I've got my paper round pay to come and I daren't have too much cash at home.' She leant forward, kissed me on the cheek. 'Thanks again,' she said and rode off. I put the notes with her receipt and stared after her. No more, I said to myself, no more. I certainly wasn't spending that money, or even taking it home. I went into the Oxfam shop and pushed it into their collecting box.

Mum seemed quite upset that Jess had gone off on holiday. 'She really takes you out of yourself,' she said. 'Such a nice girl.' I said nothing. A few days later a picture postcard arrived from Italy. 'Had to flee the country but I think I've shaken them off. Am lying low and keeping an eye open for blue and white vans. Love, Jess.'

'Funny girl,' Mum said, passing it over after she'd read it. 'What's this joke about vans?' I just grunted through my toast. 'Play your cards right, Dan, and they might invite you to go with them another time. Be good for your Italian.' Ending up in an Italian prison would certainly do something for my Italian I thought, but I didn't say anything. I spent a lot of time walking on Port Meadow, and reading. Somehow the days seemed long. We couldn't afford a holiday this year, but I had a week with Gran, who always spoils me.

A few days before term began I answered the phone and heard Jess's voice. 'Dan, I've got this brilliant plan. Meet me at the café in half an hour. How are you?'

I thought of her receipt hidden in one of my books upstairs. This was the moment I had been planning for months, the moment when I could finally turn on her, have her at my mercy. 'Hold on a moment,' I say and run upstairs. I take out the receipt and run downstairs and pick up the phone. 'Hello,' I say, 'are you still there? I want to read you something I'm holding in my hand.' I read it out to Jess. Horrified silence comes out of the phone as she realizes the full implications. 'Shall I send this to your Inspector Mopper?' I ask. There's no answer from the phone. 'I think that's stalemate,' I say. 'We're equal. It's finished. Goodbye for ever, Jess,' I say.

'Are you still there, Dan?' she asked.

'Yes,' I said. 'Yes, I'll be there.'